Also by A. G. Mojtabai
MUNDOME

The 400 Eels of Sigmund Freud

A.G. Mojtabai

SIMON AND SCHUSTER   NEW YORK

DESIGNED BY ELIZABETH WOLL
MANUFACTURED IN THE UNITED STATES OF AMERICA

1   2   3   4   5   6   7   8   9   10

LIBRARY OF CONGRESS CATALOGING IN PUBLICATION DATA

MOJTABAI, A. G. 1937–
      THE 400 EELS OF SIGMUND FREUD.

      I. TITLE.
PZ4.M715FO [PS3563.O374]   813'.5'4   76–1987
ISBN 0–671–22248–1

ACKNOWLEDGMENTS

I am grateful to A. Alvarez and Nan Talese for criticism and encouragement in the right proportions. Marlin Demlinger and Martin W. Helgesen, librarians at the City College of New York, were helpful in the search for recalcitrant factual material.

Free, very free adaptations have been made of materials from Alex Comfort's *The Biology of Senescence* (Rinehart & Co., 1956), George R. Geiger's *John Dewey in Perspective* (Oxford University Press, 1958), and Phillip R. White's *The Cultivation of Animal and Plant Cells* (2nd ed., Ronald Press, 1963). I have taken the greatest liberties with details throughout. To name one of many instances: the student projects all bear the stamp of work done at the beginning of the fifties, while Dr. Alkavist's model of DNA would have been later. What I am after is emblematic, not literal, truth.

To my parents
Naomi and Robert Alpher

The characters in this story are fictional, meaning that each is a mosaic mix of many individuals, some imagined, some known. The chain of events is imaginary, a thought-experiment, what might have, could have, happened if . . . But it all began in recollection.

There was a group such as this; for two summers I was part of it. And the Four Winds is standing today under another name. The program which it houses is one of the landmarks in the field of educational innovation. The program has undergone many relaxations and liberalizing changes over the years, although it has never ceased to produce a solid core of distinguished biologists, biochemists and doctors—among them two Nobel laureates. In ways diverse and strange, it has also left its mark upon the rest of us.

A.G.M.
Yaddo, 1975

Two Jews walk about, an inseparable pair—one inquirer and one responder, and the one keeps asking, but the other keeps evading and evading, and there's no way for them to part.

—OSIP MANDELSTAM, *Fourth Prose*
(trans. by Clarence Brown)

1

It's an old movie she plays sleeping or waking. Isaiah is the only star. Special effects—Isaiah, sound—Isaiah, lighting, a light without modulation—*his*. There isn't much of a plot. He stands on the edge of a high wall; defiant, he holds his ground; it is narrow ground, pitched exceedingly high.

Then—without warning, he lets go. A student of physics, she stands by and watches him fall: per second per second.

It's too late to undo anything. Even the ritual of return has been closed to her. Once, in summer, finding herself in the neighborhood of the estate, she drives past the Four Winds. She follows the narrow road as it meanders and twists, keeping a steady speed, then lurches to a halt. A trespasser's warning is chained to the gate.

Except for the sign, everything seems as it was on the

day she first came. The same gate: an iron gate with teeth. The road still unpaved. A sense, clearer now than before, of having come to the land's end. She can hear the clanking of old iron; it must be the buoy near the Cormorant, the familiar bell tolling its only note. One. One. One.

More than ten years have gone by and nothing has changed. The same early dusk, the same rain.

It's too late.

Eleven years ago, they'd pressed themselves into the tiny station wagon waiting at the airport. They were crammed to capacity; there was the hired driver, Naomi, five or six other students, and all their luggage. One boy with an expensive tennis racket had been considerate enough to stash his treasure on top of the luggage in the trunk, so there was some resentment when Isaiah refused to relinquish his violin and sat clutching it, taking up more space than anyone else.

"Must be priceless," someone whispered.

There was no response.

Louder: "I'm sure that's a priceless piece of scientific equipment."

"It is to me," said Isaiah without a touch of humor.

They let the matter drop.

Naomi switched her attention to what was passing outside; she had never seen so many kinds of trees. One of the boys began reeling off the names—spruce, hemlock, hornbeam and beech, maple, hoop ash, birch, hackmatack, poplar and pine. . . . It grew dark, not by degrees, but all at once, as if they had entered a grove.

A car approached them and, in the beam of the head-lights, Naomi made a closer study of Isaiah. He looked ashen, but everyone did in that light. On close inspection, his cheeks seemed cobbled. Acne, most likely, but a bad case. He sat well forward, hunched over his precious fiddle, his mouth thin as a thread. For some reason—his isolation, maybe, or his stiffness, his determination *not* to please—he reminded Naomi of a boy named Sam she used to know back in the days when she went to Hebrew school, in the early grades. Sam was usually quiet. His one claim to fame was that, every year, he'd be the only one to volunteer to act the part of Haman in the Purim play. Absolutely no one offered to play the traitor Haman. Hands shot up for Mordecai, for Esther—but never for Haman, that was a firm tradition.

She'd had her fill of that, of morality plays with their everlasting victims and executioners—stick figures, not real people. Naomi prided herself on her realism; she had no patience for moral simplifications.

It began to rain. Only a few hours before, it had been summer; now it felt like late autumn. The light was gone from the sky. Naomi shivered as she folded her arms across her chest for warmth. If Isaiah had leaned back, there might have been less draft on her side. She stared out the window: the trees continued, darker now. Then the solitary sign—NITE CRAWLERS—a beacon in the gloom.

"Night crawlers . . . that's a kind of fishing bait," Isaiah explained. "I saw this before. Yeah. This is North country. I should have brought my mittens." He persisted in making remarks about the scenery they were passing, how much it looked like Nova Scotia, where he'd gone to visit a pen pal two summers before. One of the great events in his life. As soon as he began to speak, Naomi knew he was from Brooklyn: "I sore this" gave him away at once. Flatbush, was it? Home ground, they were neighbors. She had a special feeling for Isaiah right from the start. It was more embarrassment than anything else.

No one was interested in where Isaiah had been two summers before. There was a heavy silence in the back of the car, broken only when an anonymous stomach grumbled. They went on, the rain heavier as they went. They moved slowly, feeling the way with long lights. Sometime later they hit a different kind of road. It was narrow and rough.

In front of them: an iron gate with teeth. The driver opened the car door, muttering at the wet, and stepped out. The rain slashed at his face, his shoulders, his hands. The gate must have been heavy; it gave with an aching sound.

"Keep your eye peeled!"

Wheels churned, spinning gravel. They entered a private driveway. "A mansion," someone whispered, "the real thing."

But Naomi couldn't see the house properly. They'd come upon it too suddenly. The rain and the dusk obscured all but the immediate view: a small crowd gathered on the porch. Early arrivals, eight or nine of them. One stood out in gleaming yellow oilskins, giving a glare.

The figure in the yellow slicker moved toward them.

Damp and bent with cold, Naomi wormed her way out of the car.

16

"Welcome! Welcome all of you—" the woman in yellow began. "I feel like I've known you for a long time. But you don't know me. Dr. Eloson is in charge at the Four Winds and I'm his wife. Call me Aunt Ethel."

Most of the new arrivals, Naomi among them, began by milling around the trunk end of the station wagon. There they huddled, stalling, as though nothing mattered more than sorting out their luggage, and no one was more dear to them than their driver, whom they'd met only an hour before and who hadn't said a word but "ay-yuh" to their few questions in that time. No one wanted to be the first to step forward.

But, one by one, they claimed their bags and broke away from the old group.

"Park your suitcases upstairs, just park them—I'll give you fifteen minutes. There'll be time tomorrow to unpack," Aunt Ethel announced. "Come back down to the common room right away—we'll get properly acquainted after a snack. First of all I want you to check in with Mr. Homay, the nice man with the clipboard."

Mr. Homay waved his hand gaily. "Call me Bob," he shouted.

"Don't forget now—fifteen minutes." Aunt Ethel released them.

The new arrivals lined up.

If Mr. Homay wasn't a gym teacher, he should have been. He was wearing a billed cap, sweat shirt, Bermuda shorts, sneakers, even a steel whistle on a chain.

"Naomi Heschel, let's see . . ." Mr. Homay's finger moved down the list. "Ah, here we are. East Eleven. Your roommate will be coming up tomorrow." He smiled hard.

"Heard all about you. You're our youngest—fourteen, aren't you?"

Does it show that much? Naomi wondered. She assured him that she was fifteen plus—plus half a week, though she'd been younger when she made her application.

"Fourteen or fifteen—you're still our youngest. We're expecting great things of you, great things," he said warmly. "It's going to be a beautiful summer."

2

"GREAT THINGS OF YOU . . ." She stepped
over the threshold. A boy offered to lend her a hand with
her luggage, but Naomi insisted she could manage on her
own and began toiling up the staircase. It was a grand
curving structure, the kind she'd seen only in magazines
and romantic Civil War films. But this one was un-
carpeted, the banisters were loose and ticked as she
climbed.

Her suitcase was very heavy; she paused on the landing
and peered down at the foyer. The anteroom with its
gleaming parquet floor, the hallway, everywhere Naomi
looked was grand, spacious, utterly bare—stripped of all
furniture and ornaments, the shell of a once-great house.

East 11: her room was cell-like and cold. The light
from an unshaded bulb overhead was dazzling. The floorboards rattled. There was a window, but it framed nothing. There were two iron cots, a thin striped mattress

doubled over on each, a U.S. Navy blanket folded on top of that. A chest of drawers in unvarnished wood, a stool, a basin, that was all.

Naomi unfolded the mattress. It was old, with rust stains. She would have to ask for sheets. The bureau drawers were empty; the closet contained nothing but wire hangers. A hospital room after a removal might look like this. What was missing to make it home? Warmth, mess, noise, congestion, life—everything.

Only a few minutes to spare. First she creamed her elbows and her knees. This was her one beautification ritual and absolutely essential, for her elbows were crusty and her knees were nubbly as tweed, full of tiny bumps from hairs that never surfaced. She slipped on a heavy sweater and managed to dig out a pair of pajamas and a comb. A bell rang—she still hadn't located her toothbrush. She heard the others, a small army trampling past. She switched off the light and followed.

They gathered in the large common room on the first floor. There was a stone fireplace in the middle of one wall. It had been bricked up to keep out bats. The room was full of mismatched porch chairs, basket chairs and split-log benches, a single stuffed armchair in skirts, and long stretches of bare board between. Along the far wall, a great number of wooden folding chairs were stacked in a row. They looked ancient.

Little groups were forming, none in Naomi's vicinity. On a wicker table nearby she spotted a stack of phonograph records. She went over to examine them.

"Interested in music?" Isaiah sidled up.

"Sometimes," she said. "It depends."

"What do they have here? William Tell—Side Three . . . The Jolly Brothers Galop? They got to be kidding!"

As Isaiah shuffled through the stack, Naomi slipped off.

The others were following Mr. Homay into the kitchen. A few minutes out for milk and cake, then they'd all regroup in the reception room for the next activity—"something special."

Tertu, the cook, was introduced. She was a woman as round as she was tall. Her dress strained at the armpits: breasts to the belt. "I'm here to feed you," she said after a long pause. "Help yourselves." On cue from Aunt Ethel, the students gave Tertu and her cake a round of applause.

The "something special" turned out to be charades. Everyone agreed they were dismal. First name, last name, hometown. Those students who already knew one another were honor-bound to sit in silence.

Naomi dreaded her turn. Luckily, she was over with it early. And she didn't do too badly, since no one did very well. She got past the first part of her name easily enough.

First syllable: "Nay!" With sharp sweeps of her arms, she refused an imaginary suitor kneeling at her feet. The gesture was too abrupt and, at the same time, too trivial. Someone proposed "Scat!" And tittered, knowing full well you couldn't begin a name with it. "Go!" "Out!" "Begone!" followed in a wake of silliness. Then, out of thin air, by inspiration or cheating, came the right syllable.

Next: "Oh, me!" She rounded her lips and made a caricature of exclaiming: hands raised in surrender, mouth like a bottletop. The students flailed around for a couple of minutes. Until a boy in the middle of the room began waving his hand wildly. He had hair that was almost white. "Nay-oh-my!" he shouted out. And another voice said it in one breath. Close enough.

On to Heschel. "He"—by pointing at a boy. Then "shell"—she snatched it from the floor, shaped it in her palm, cupped it to her ear—nothing easier. "Brooklyn" was surefire. All she needed was "brook"—fingers rippling keyboard scales on a low piano that barely cleared the floor. And it was over. Any others from Brooklyn or Brookline would have to scrounge for themselves. What would Isaiah use? Naomi wondered about that, briefly. She glanced around the room for him. He was sitting off to one side in a far corner, as if hoping, by some lucky oversight, not to be called upon. Isaiah Yettman—with a name like his it would not be easy.

Someone was standing in the doorway waiting for Naomi to finish her routine. After she'd made her way back to her seat, he strode to the front of the room. Naomi examined him with the greatest interest. He had a considerable tan for so early in the summer. Dressed in a tennis sweater, white ducks and white shoes, he reminded her of a man she'd seen repeatedly in an ad for expensive whisky. He had long legs, his hair was close-cut and graying. The effect of casual and mindless elegance was spoiled by thick glasses and misty, evanescent eyes. He began to speak.

"I'm Dr. Eloson—Frank Eloson, to be exact." A forceful bass voice. "Let's cut the formality. You can call me Chief. I know every one of you." As he spoke, his hands moved—allemande right, allemande left. They were hands worth looking at, broad in the palms, long fingers with spatulate tips, and perfectly manicured nails with perfectly regular moons.

He greeted the students as "the future leaders of American science, the biologists of tomorrow." Out of hundreds of applications from bright high-school students all over the country, this tiny group had been screened and selected. He knew how capable they were and, as an educator, he also knew that capabilities had to be nourished or they would atrophy. "That's my function here— to nourish," he repeated. "My wife and I—we've been living at the Four Winds for more than a week now. Let me tell you: it's been a dead house. But tonight the house is full of life. Enjoy it, enjoy this evening, it's the last bit of play for a while. By Monday we'll be in full gear—all business. If any of you feel the slightest pang of homesickness, see me. I've got a cure for it. It's called work, the fascination of hard work. You'll see what I mean—"

He went on to introduce Aunt Ethel and Mr. Homay as though they'd just materialized, and to explain that Mrs. Homay was upstairs putting her children to bed.

"Ship's in good hands," he concluded. "We're ready to cast off."

On with the charades. Isaiah was last; it was nearly ten-thirty before they got to him. Everyone must be tired of the game by now, he argued. Why not save time and simply state his name?

Aunt Ethel was quick to respond: "Oh, no, no exceptions. Everybody's done it, done the best they could."

"That's just it," said Isaiah, "it's all been done. I can't think of anything new."

"Oh, come on, try. Sure you can do it." Aunt Ethel beamed encouragement. "Each of you was selected for your originality above all. Don't disappoint us now. Just try."

So Isaiah thought hard while the room stirred with small sounds. The lateness of the hour, by itself, would have doomed anyone's best effort.

At last, with a hush, it began.

"I"—pointing to himself.

"Say"—silent gapings, teeth snappings and grindings. He seemed to be chewing something that wouldn't give. They exhausted all the eating words. He made a megaphone of his cupped hands. The students worked down in intensity from "rally," "scream," "shout," to "speak." After great effort, one of the girls came up with "says," and Isaiah gestured rapidly with come-hither motions to show how warm she was. She hesitated: "said? say?"

"A"—one lifted finger. No response. Then he formed the letter A with three fingers. That was easy enough.

"Yet"—he shrugged and shrugged, to no effect.

"Man"—again he pointed to himself. No one considered the intended syllable, for Isaiah was clearly not yet a man. "I," "me," "myself," "human," "sternum," "self," "who"—the students gave up rapidly; they were long past caring.

"You could have put more effort into it," said Aunt Ethel as Isaiah passed her on his way out. "I *know* you could have done better."

"I really hate games," Isaiah explained. "Don't know why. Seems like I always did."

They formed a line in the hall before going up. Aunt Ethel and Mr. Homay wheeled in a large hamper and began distributing sheets and pillowcases. They were new and cold.

3

THE MORNING BEGAN with three bells. Finishing her unpacking was the first order of business. Once her luggage was stashed in the basement, Naomi was free to wander the grounds. It was good to see the sun after the gloom of the basement. She felt proud of her efficiency; not one of the other students was free yet.

She took a path around the garden, skirting a row of vine frets. But there were no vines, nothing but weed and grass sprouting thickly around the bases of the poles. There was a small lettuce bed, a mint patch, a row of runner beans, the frazzled heads of what might have been carrots. That seemed to be all in the way of cultivation. She spotted a gardener in khakis with a wheelbarrow. His back to her, he was busy blowing his nose between two fingers and wiping them on the grass. Much the best way, Naomi thought as she slipped past. Ecology and all.

The air was so fresh, it stung. There was pine in it, juniper and salt. She turned right where the path forked, aiming for the bluffs on the ocean side of the grounds. The path entered a grove and seemed to lose itself around a clump of heaped stones. No, the stones formed a marker, she could see that now. There must have been some storms recently: a number of trees leaned against their neighbors. A tall pine lay in the debris of its own branches, its massive roots exposed, still twisting into the earth.

A chipmunk, skittering toward her, gave a little shriek and disappeared into the brush. She could smell the ocean clearly now. The path ended. She found herself out on an escarpment, fronting the sea. She noticed with disappointment that someone was here before her and seemed to be comfortably perched.

It was Isaiah, reading a book. He looked up briefly and waved.

Determined to find a lookout of her own, Naomi made her way along the rock ledge, until it became sheer cliff, impassable. On her belly, she inched her way over to the edge of the bluffs and held there, just her chin hanging over. The cliff dropped sheer below for about twenty feet, then there was a substantial ledge, a gull-spattered love seat for three. Then sheer drop again, right down into the sea. Not a friendly sea: gray above, black beneath, level and somnolent, unwarmed by the sun.

A little before lunchtime everyone gathered on the front lawn for group photographs. Mr. Homay had set up his camera on a tripod and was walking from person to person taking meter readings. The Homay children squatted front row center. It was the first time Noami had seen Mrs. Homay, but no one took the trouble of introducing her. She was either unfriendly or very shy. Mr. Homay asked her to take off her sunglasses for the picture, but she shook her head no, and he didn't press the point.

Naomi had not yet chosen her place. She stood out in front, watching the group assemble and testing herself as to how many names she could remember.

Chief stood between Aunt Ethel and Mrs. Homay, an arm around each of their waists. Naomi took a long look at the three of them. Mrs. Homay was clearly the younger of the two women. In her baggy slacks and what must have been one of her husband's pullovers, she was also much the plainer. She had a comfortable shape, not fat, but generous, ample. Her hair was "dishwater blond." She had a full face, a childish snub nose, and a saddle of freckles over nose and cheeks.

Aunt Ethel was smaller and finer in build, and in every way more intense. Her face was very pale, set off against jet-black hair. She had a straight nose, continuous in profile from brow to tip. Naomi had only seen a nose like that once, in a classic Greek frieze; she'd been certain it was an exaggeration.

Aunt Ethel could have been beautiful and might have been at one time. But now she narrowed her eyes against the light; there was a sharp furrow between her brows, and steep, etched lines on either side of her mouth.

She wore a pale-blue gingham blouse and freshly ironed denims with knife creases. All very crisp. Her sneakers were of a stunning whiteness. It was a holiday outfit but worn with a severe, rather cold, correctness.

Chief stood alongside, relaxed and smiling. At least Naomi thought he was smiling. His mouth was, but it was hard to know what his eyes were doing under those thick glasses. Chief and Aunt Ethel both seemed older in the morning than they had the night before; they seemed to be in their late forties. Chief's ruddiness looked less wholesome in the daylight. Still, he was gorgeous and knew it. He was dressed in a yachtsman's outfit, a theme in white and blue. Unlike his wife, he managed to look informal and festive. Naomi found a place in the row behind him and noticed he was grasping Mrs. Homay's waist quite strongly, while his other arm hung like a slack belt over Aunt Ethel's hip.

"You'll have to come forward," Mr. Homay called. Naomi was quite eclipsed behind the adults. Reluctantly, she stepped out, settling in the first row beside the Homay children.

Still—it wasn't right. Isaiah strung out too far in the third row. "No one's going to eat you, fella—move in," Mr. Homay urged. "Okay, everybody. Smile—say *cheese.*"

Naomi blinked and set her mouth firm. She'd be damned if she'd say "cheese" on cue.

"Fine. For the next shot, I want you all to say *money.*" Mrs. Homay seemed to flinch every time her husband spoke.

He's making a perfect ass of himself, thought Naomi, and he doesn't even know it.

Smiling, mostly smiling, they froze in place.

4

CHIEF AND AUNT ETHEL both dressed for supper that first evening, although they ate in their own dining room with only themselves for company. Chief had on a white dinner jacket, and Aunt Ethel wore a striped linen suit, stockings and white pumps.

The Elosons certainly kept up appearances. By now, all the students had been out to the garage behind the Mouse House to take a look at their car. It was a cream-colored Mercedes; the upholstery was black leather, and the license plate read "FRATHEL" for their combined names.

The social hour at nine that evening began with a brief announcement. Aunt Ethel came in carrying a small metal box with a slot in the top. "This is the suggestion box," she said, holding it up for general inspection. "You might wonder why we need a suggestion box here, but the fact is some people are shyer than others and find it hard to speak up. Here's your way of making criticisms freely without that kind of fear. Tertu will keep the key, so nobody's going to raid it. We'll open it every other week to start. Let's not forget. It'll be right here on the little table. And, no, we will *not* serve beer on Saturday nights —you can skip that one. Though we'll listen to any constructive suggestions you have to make."

Aunt Ethel smiled warmly. She was so friendly, so eager to be agreeable. After only one day, Naomi felt at home at the Four Winds. Her roommate, Polly Ames, had finally arrived. Naomi had taken her on a tour of the house and grounds, pointing out this and that feature, as though she'd lived in the house all her life. The other students were beginning to relax; the newness was wearing off and the tension of work had not yet begun. Only Isaiah seemed still on edge.

During the social hour, Isaiah wandered the room, forlorn. Chief tried to exchange a few words with him but quickly extricated himself. Isaiah moved from group to group, saying little and keeping his hands stuffed deep in his pockets.

A couple of students were discussing college entrance exams and turned to include him. But he answered, "Do you *care?*" with such vehemence that Naomi turned sharply. She was standing on the other side of the room near the door, chatting with Polly and Herb Smith. Naomi didn't care much for Herb, who was older than the others, back for a second summer, and very sure of himself. He was already accepted in college, headed for a career in surgery—it was all he talked about.

Isaiah passed them on his way out.

"Where you going?" Naomi intercepted.

"Out. I can't stand the silence."

"Silence? That what you call this racket?"

"The silence of people talking a mile a minute. A kind of roaring suction."

A few minutes later, lights went on in the adjoining lecture hall, followed by the sounds of a vigorous tuning-up.

All conversation died away; an amazed hush had fallen over the room. Aunt Ethel, who'd been passing by, stopped dead in her tracks. She glanced from side to side as if trying to remember her route.

Then Chief did something strange. He cocked his ear, stared pointedly at Aunt Ethel, and chuckled.

"A calling card," he said.

"A childish bid for attention," said Aunt Ethel.

Naomi didn't follow; it was like a conversation in code.

Whatever it meant, their communication didn't last long. Chief looked elsewhere; Aunt Ethel stepped forward. Voices resumed, mounting in competition with the fiddle.

"He's homesick," Aunt Ethel explained to Herb, and to anyone else who might be listening. "That's all there is to it. The less attention we pay—the less said of it—the better."

Two flights up, Anna Homay was listening. In spite of the rain, in spite of the fact that she was having herself a good cry, she could make out a subdued commotion below. The voices ran together and, once in a while, a single voice rose above the rest.

She'd been crying when the second group of students arrived the night before. Giving herself a good soaking, as Bob said. Feeling sorry for herself, setting a bad example —all true.

Susie was sound asleep, and Jim was beginning to doze at last. It had grown cold so suddenly. Anna sat in darkness, studying the fanlight over the door, reviewing the day past. The children had been cooped up since early morning and had abandoned, in turn, jacks, Nok Hockey, Hi-Lo, a jigsaw puzzle—one of those thousand-piece misfortunes, of which thirty were linked and the rest scattered.

When at last they were drawing quietly, Anna had decided she could safely leave them on their own for a minute. She carried the empty suitcases down to the basement.

Returning, Anna lost her way. The corridor she was following led nowhere. Much of the house was still a mystery to her. A sharp left—and she entered a room full of twilight, so dim that for a moment she could make out nothing. It was a small room, no bigger than a closet, lined with shelves. The shelves were ranged with pickling jars, full of what seemed to be vintage cauliflower. Foibles of the rich.

Was that red pepper? That jar on the second shelf.

She groped for a switch. What came to light startled her: a rich array of nature's mistakes. None of it was new, the formaldehyde was muddy, what should have been white was gray, the reds were umber. Scanning, she noted a heart full of lard, one brain pickled yellow, one green; an infant with two arms, four legs and a profusion of genitals; a tapeworm folded endlessly upon itself, filling every inch of available space; a kidney studded with stones; an encysted ovary. A uterus in cross section, very full. Inside: an embryo six months gone, nestling in eternal petrifaction. There was more—

She didn't want to see.

The children were still drawing quietly when she returned. Little marvels, each separate and complete, ten fingers, ten toes, little knowing what a narrow escape . . . She decided to capitalize on the peace. Settling heavily on the bed, she reached for her latest *Women's Gala*. It was plump with ads.

Ten minutes later Aunt Ethel was at the door: Would Anna lend Tertu a hand at getting lunch on the table? As if there were a choice. Anna brought the children down with her. Luckily there was something to occupy them in the kitchen, a mynah bird, whose name must have been Larry, for the first thing he said was:

"Good morning Larry."

The Homay children were delighted; they shouted out their names.

"Whoopee!" said Larry. "Naughty boy!"

Anna studied him closely.

"What you doin'?" He crooked his neck, viewing her on a slant. "Just looking," said Anna, "do you mind?" He was smaller than a parrot, glossy black with yellow earmuffs. "Holy smoke!" he said. Anna peered intently into the gleaming pellet eyes—they gave back no image, nothing.

"How are you?" she asked.

"Stay tuned," he replied.

It was quite chilling, every bit as chilling as those pickling jars. In spite of the bare fact before her very eyes, Anna kept looking for a tiny hidden man, a diminished ventriloquist as the only possible source of that sound. Or a talking doll, the kind you squeezed. But, no, it was much more complicated: Larry spoke with the precise diction of a recorded phone message. The part that made her queasy was the lilt, the touch of some regionalism. His voice was a perfect facsimile of a human voice, perfect, and at the same time, perfectly empty.

"Where do you come from, Larry?" she asked, trying to place the accent. "Where's home?"

But Larry didn't answer.

She walked away, across the room to the drainboard, to pick up some more dishes.

"Stop that!" from Larry. "Will you stop that?" Then silence.

The situation deteriorated rapidly after this. The children began to tap at the wires of the cage, trying to make the bird say "Holy smoke!" over again. They jostled the base until Larry began to respond, emitting a stream of shrieks. Then Tertu was forced to pull down the velvet cover and, when that didn't work, to carry the cage upstairs.

No sooner accomplished than Jim provoked Susie into chanting, "I must clean my city shoes," faster and faster each time. They roared with laughter as they picked up speed, until Tertu said: "I'd wash their mouths out with soap for that, I would."

Anna said nothing. It was easy enough for Tertu to give advice, a spinster who lived by herself, without children or grandchildren. The two women went in to set the tables, silence heavy between them, broken only by the clashing of silver.

After lunch, the children napped. It was late afternoon when Aunt Ethel called them down for some help in weeding the garden. For Jim and Susie, it wasn't such a bad idea, it turned out to be a diversion, but Anna deeply resented being called. She failed to see how her unpaid labor around the house constituted a fringe benefit to Bob's meager salary. Bob was hired as statistician, counselor and photographer. He was promised "ideal conditions for family summering" at no extra cost as one of many added attractions. They'd be living in a thirty-room mansion, the Elosons wrote, windows on all sides, open to the four winds and fronting the sea. A brochure full of alluring photos had been sent to the Homays. It all looked grand and palatial. Naturally, no mention was made of the fact that the Homays' portion of the mansion would be three tiny rooms under the eaves; that these rooms had windows on one side only; and that they could expect to sizzle when the heat peaked.

Summer by the sea, the Elosons had written, a private beach. The "beach" was like no other she had seen: a few twisted jack pines, a rugged outcropping of cliff and stone which tumbled down, straight down, into the sea. "Very interesting, geologically speaking," said Bob, swallowing his disappointment, "most interesting. I bet you don't realize that the shearing of these cliffs is along fault lines and has nothing to do with the eroding power of the sea. The sea is only playing with the low-lying rubble here."

How interesting! The children couldn't possibly play in

the water; the footing was craggy and uneven, treacherous. One false step and they'd be in over their heads. And it was cold, dark water.

Anna recalled the first time the children had seen the sea. It was at Hale's Crescent, a true beach, level and sunny with warm yellow sand. Jim had never seen waves before and, having no word for them, he'd cried out: "See the water walking!" But here, at the Four Winds, the water did not walk.

Here the water leaped and hurled. Twenty or thirty yards from shore was a V-shaped ledge called the Cormorant. It broke the back of the sea and many a small boat. A buoy farther out gave warning, but often too late, judging from the heapings on the shoals. When the tide was low, Anna could catalog the wreckage: planking from traps and crates, cork, barrel hoops, tin cans, coils of net and heavy rope, siftings. At high tide, she could see the water lathering up some yards out, but that was all.

Ideal summering in a mansion by the sea . . . no expenses. Chance of a lifetime. They'd swallowed the bait, hook, line and sinker. The salary by itself was scant enough, so there *had* to be compensations. Photographs of the Four Winds were impressive and photos don't lie.

So they had packed their hopes and come.

Anna sat in the rocker, poised on the half-tilt. Perched at a crazy angle, very still. The rain blurred and bleared everything. She hated all students everywhere. It was a mood, she knew. At home, when she got like this, she'd weep for hours. Sometimes she'd sit and watch the dust gather and fall—she'd do nothing. She'd never been much of a housewife. The dust would settle like fur over sills and shelves, tables and chairs, while she did nothing but trail her finger through it.

She heard the cheerful voices below, Bob's false-hearty, mixing and blending, boosting all the rest. That was the saddest sound of all and, she couldn't help it, fresh tears welled up. All for a little cash, their lives were cramped and bent. They were being used, used.

Then the voices broke and fell away, as if on the brink of some catastrophe. What was it?

The sound of a fiddle, rippling, rushing, a river swelling, putting to rout everything that stood to hold it back.

She listened.

5

"It's a sagging time," Naomi had written home. That was on Wednesday of the first week. "Nice here," she explained, "though nothing really scientific has happened yet. It seems as if we're busy with everything but."

Housework was elaborate and time-consuming, something she hadn't expected. There were more than twenty rooms in the Four Winds, and some of the larger ones had been partitioned. It would take the students a full week to return to starting point on their sweeping, scrubbing, dusting, oiling. The students were divided into work crews with three members in each; the crews would change jobs every week. Naomi mapped her summer: dishes, woodwork, furniture, floors, laundry, Mouse House, Rabbit House, dishes again, woodwork again. "The house shines," she noted, "but who's it for?"

Monday morning they'd started on their course of "Basics," ten general assignments required of all students.

Except for the first two, Basics could be carried out any time during the summer, at the student's convenience. In most cases, they were small matters involving simple, standard techniques. "We're moving from the known to the known," Naomi wrote, filled with a deep impatience.

Most of the students shared her feeling. Basics were "baby stuff," suitable for high school or college, at best. They all felt themselves ready for postgraduate work and dreamed of their own experiments, solo projects, to be carried out at the Four Winds, but under the sponsorship of senior researchers at Spemann Lab. They had come for sponsors; the summer was to be "an apprenticeship in scientific research"; this was what the program was all about. They wanted to do so much, and they had so little time.

Monday, Tuesday, Wednesday—they seemed to be marching in place, in lockstep. Their first assignment was dissection, comparison of the gross anatomy of rabbit, guinea pig and mouse. The students were required to make detailed colored drawings as they went along, which slowed them down considerably.

No textbooks were allowed. Chief stayed with them the first morning only, then excused himself. He was busy setting up the operating room. Mr. Homay continued to make the rounds in Chief's place, answering what questions he could, always with the disclaimer that this sort of thing wasn't his cup of tea. He was a statistician and accustomed to what he called "clean work," which this clearly wasn't.

What Naomi remembered best from that time were the blood spatters on her lab coat, like showers of dark wheat—that and the prickle of formaldehyde in her nostrils, sour and sharp. They worked in a converted garage, though the weather was fine, sun out and everything drenched in light.

Sometime during the second afternoon, they moved onto picnic tables in the sun; they spread newspapers and carried everything out. They had to work faster this way— organs dried up and changed color—and the flies were a nuisance. But you could smell the grass, and the dead animals looked less dead, more like split fruits.

Naomi shared a table with her roommate, Polly Ames, Eddy Bartusek and Tom Li. Tom was the most skillful. He had a way of undressing the animal, spreading a center seam from "gulch to zilch" as though he'd found a zipper in the skin.

They concocted gourmet dishes.

"*Specialités gastronomiques,*" Eddy began with a flourish. "Sebaceous broth," he suggested, "for a starter."

"Omelette cum haustra," Alex Nesselroth continued.

"Pâté mesogaster," said Polly.

"Pickled ampulla of Vater," offered her neighbor, Leo Proudhon.

"Ugh!" cried Jenise Bunsen.

"Salad with vibrissae." Eddy again. "That'll tickle your taste buds."

"I pass," said Jenise.

"Pancreas in mesenterial nest—how does that sound?" said Hans Tivonen.

"Saddle of spleen on toast," Naomi temporized. She tried to visualize the dish with parsley and trimmings.

"Tonsils in syrup," chirped Tom Li.

41

"I'd rather not," said Isaiah.

"Anything else?" Eddy welcomed further suggestions. Vito and Johnny shrugged, no help from there.

"How about rose water in finger bowl, seasoned to taste?" Stevie Conroy brought the menu to an elegant close.

Then it was down to business. Slowly, in her careful back-slant, Naomi wrote:

In all three animals, the sternum was first palpated and a mid-ventral incision was made from the sternum to the pubic symphysis. A similar incision was also extended laterally along the lower edge of the rib cage so that it fell on top of the previously retracted skin layer. . . .

"You're the expert—how do you figure on writing it up?" Isaiah approached Tom Li.

"Haven't started yet. But Naomi's already at it."

Upon request, Naomi offered up her model prose.

"What a peculiar handwriting! The letters all tilt backwards like they're afraid of touching—I bet that means something."

"Latent or blatant," said Eddy, "everything *means.* Freud . . . Whatever you think you are, you are that other thing. You're guilty in either case. You can't win."

Isaiah read the short paragraph twice, mouthing the words silently. "That's stately prose there, Naom," he conceded. "*Molto calmo, sempre legatissimo.* Wait till you come to tying up the tubes so the shit stays put—'a ligature was applied'—yeah? I get the picture, thanks." And off he went to write an unexpurgated version.

Naomi read over what she had written and couldn't help admiring it; she found it exemplary, a thoroughly professional lead-off. She continued:

In the rabbit and guinea pig the esophagus was located and a ligature applied. The tube was cut above the ligature and the anterior section of the digestive system was freed from the surrounding mesentery.

Her favorite, for some reason, was the respiratory system. She'd crack open the thoracic dome, neatly, like a walnut on the half-shell, and, snipping through the intercostal muscle, find everything sweet reasonableness within, all symmetry and balance. The little corpses were in mint condition, the lungs flushed and pearly.

The digestive system was less inspiring; they moved from fundus through pylorus, via the smooth small intestine, the bulbar caecum, up the rhythmic ascending colon, and down. The students were required to stretch out the entire length of intestine and to measure it. Once unpacked, the long coils never could be squeezed back into the narrow spaces from which they came. Tom Li tried it on a dare and made an awful mess.

The reproductive system was close work. They had to double up, for less than a third of their group had males. The urinary system followed, from the renal arteries to the urethra. It looked like delicate embroidery in the mouse, so fine.

They did what they could with the circulatory system, from jugular to femoral. What remained of the animals looked like the wrecked hulls of boats, row upon row of plundered casks, and the white lab coats of the students were bright as butchers' smocks, steeped in gore. Eddy kept ribbing Naomi: "What's a nice girl like you doing in a place like this?"

But Naomi wasn't nice, and dissection was nothing new to her. She'd started before her tenth year. Clumsily, entirely on her own. There'd never been anything pure about her curiosity, she was under no illusions on that score. It was the same impulse that drove children to fumble with themselves in the dark. What was the dirty secret?

Why the elaborate precautions to keep dying under wraps and death six feet down and stoned over?

There was no afterlife, that was the only straight answer she got. What then? Something about "dust" and "the spirit." It was "spirit" that troubled her most: if you couldn't see it, or hear it, or touch it, then what *was* it?

The answer was always the same: she would understand when she was older. Naomi couldn't wait; the evasions made her dizzy and everything unreal. For the ashes of pogroms and camps were raked over continually in her hearing, but the death of anyone she knew was unmentionable. Why?

There'd been too many deaths around her and all of them so carefully missed. Hocus pocus: grandfather, aunt, baby brother, all in one year. When her brother failed to come home from the hospital, Naomi decided to stir up some "dust," to investigate the dead mouse she'd discovered in the basement laundry room. She went down to meet him, armed only with her mother's manicure set.

Studying the tiny, wizened body made something come to her throat. But Naomi's mind was made up. With the help of nail scissors, file, tweezers and orange stick, she snipped open the rib cage. Her methods were rudimentary: pinch, poke, lift, grope.

She was amazed at the order she found. Afterwards, her feelings were different: she'd solved no riddles, of course, "the spirit" had eluded her, but she'd mastered some of her fear. From then on, she opened up everything that came her way—a sparrow, a squirrel, a bat, two rats. She even brought a cat into the house, parking it temporarily in the spare sink while she tended to her homework. It stiffened there, a safe stash, until her mother noticed the upraised paws and there was a scene. She bought inner organs, hearts, lungs, kidneys and brains, from the butcher, spending a few pennies for each and dissecting them on plates in the kitchen, making sure she had removed all traces before her mother came home from work.

Once she opened up an earthworm and was so in the habit of amazement that she mistook the crop and gizzard for two hearts. She was set to rights only as she moved down segment by segment. An earthworm seemed to have everything a creature could want and then some, including both testes and ovaries, but no brains.

For the first few days at the Four Winds, Naomi was at a loss for many of the students' names. A few individuals made their mark on first or second contact. Isaiah made

45

his at first sight. Within the first week, Naomi could do an impersonation of him that any one of the students would recognize, using no more than five expressions:

"Who knows?"

"But why? It doesn't have to be."

"It's conceivable."

"Other things being equal—"

"Isn't that the greatest piece of thrilling music?" This last was a giveaway.

Second in distinctness was Jerome Marten, a shy, wispy boy who went to Exeter and came from the suburbs of Boston. He was easy to pick out because he stuttered. He was unforgettable because he'd paired up with Naomi on the second Basic. They'd been assigned to do a battery of blood tests on one another. Partners were decided by lot. Naomi found it easy enough to apply a tourniquet and to withdraw a syringeful of blood from Jerome's arm. Her hands were steady and sure. But when she held out her arm in turn, she noticed that Jerome's hands were trembling. He jabbed her repeatedly and muttered excuses: the vein was too small, too hard to find. A brute would have been kinder. In the end, she found the place herself, all but blacking out in the process. It was immeasurably different, working on oneself. Blood roared in her ears, her heart lurched. She drove the needle home, but hadn't the dexterity or courage to pull the plunger. Jerome hadn't the stomach for this either and called Herb over to give emergency aid.

Herb Smith acted as Chief's assistant; he was a Texan, big and brazen, more knowledgeable than Bob Homay, but much less pleasant. He'd been invited back to spend a

46

summer doing experimental surgery. With Chief, he was trying to perfect a lung-transplant technique on dogs.

Joel Rosen, a chess buff, was distinguished by sheer obnoxiousness. He talked too much. He was from Philadelphia. The girls presented no problem; there were just four in all. Jenise Bunsen, Polly Ames, Eva Probst. Naomi took an instant dislike to Evie—the kind of girl who wore sneakers with pointed toes and drowned herself in mimosa scent. Evie was from Abilene, Kansas. Naomi gave it to be understood that Oskaloosa, Abilene and Walla Walla were all one to her. She played up being a New York girl for all it was worth. After the evening of charades passed and was forgotten, she avoided mentioning Brooklyn, which was not quite Manhattan.

The other students still merged in Naomi's mind. Vito Giambri and Johnny Mendez continued as a twosome. They were both short and dark and avoided the girls.

The Homays and the Elosons were very different. Naomi never had any trouble remembering staff names. She puzzled over something she'd heard, that Aunt Ethel's real name was Edith Eloson. Naomi never got to the bottom of that rumor, who started it, or why. It was the sort of thing that flourished in defiance of logic and common sense. A mystery. In the end, Naomi concluded that it had no basis whatsoever in fact. Why would anyone want to be called "Aunt Ethel" if she had a perfectly decent name like Edith? Unless she wanted to feel a family connection with the students, for she had no family of her own. That would account for the "Aunt" part. But why "Ethel" unless her name was Ethel?

The Homays were more straightforward. They kept to

their own names and their own humdrum ways. They were plain people, they made no effort to be anything else.

Absolutely unique and immediately distinguishable in any surroundings was Dr. Alkavist, director of H. Spemann Lab. Aunt Ethel, with her precise sense of hierarchy, introduced him as "Chief's Chief." He was an ancient, nearing eighty. Jerome nicknamed him "the Alkahest," for universal solvent, and the name stuck.

The summer program for pre-college students was the Alkahest's personal brainchild. The Four Winds had been his summer home. It seemed strange, then, that he came so infrequently, that he chose not to enter into the lives of the students, but preferred to remain a figurehead, fundraiser and founder, and to keep the idea in motion from a distance. Perhaps his age made visits taxing.

Where were the sponsors? That was the nagging question. Spemann Lab was only a mile away, but it was a mile of silence. The lab acted as a supplier, providing specially inbred mice for Basics, but had no further role in these activities.

When would they ever get beyond Basics?

Toward the end of the first week the Four Winds seemed a place of quarantine, and the elaborate routine dissection seemed nothing but a blind, a deliberate attempt at distraction. Thursday, Friday, Saturday, sun in, sun out—it didn't matter. By week's end the staff of Spemann Lab had not yet spoken.

Out of nine precious weeks, one was already over.

6

It was one of those days.

Anna Homay started off by burning the sleeve of Bob's dress shirt, dreaming as she ironed. For no reason she could call to mind, except maybe the early morning chill, she kept remembering her friend Pete from years back, when she wasn't much older than Jim. On winter mornings they took turns warming each other in the school yard. Anna would stand with her back flush to the wall and Pete would stand in front of her, making a toasty sandwich. Then they reversed positions and Anna did the same for Pete. It was all very innocent and very loving.

She took the children out to the back lawn, trying her best to avoid the dissection area. No matter how hard she worked to keep them distracted, Jim kept straying; he insisted that the students were having a picnic. They were in fact spread out all over the picnic tables in the sun, but here all resemblance to picnics ended. Then Jim caught a glimpse of his father helping one of the students and cried out to be recognized. Bob signaled Anna to get the children back into the house.

Back to their kennels. Sue wanted to visit the mynah bird, but he was hidden away somewhere in the Eloson's private quarters. There was no chance of remaining on the ground floor. Even the back porch was out of bounds since the floor there was freshly waxed.

Only hours before, Anna had been dreaming of winter. But the heat had risen steadily and now their rooms were stifling.

Carrying a few coloring books, comics, jigsaw and Hi-Lo, they made their way up to the widow's walk on the roof. Jim wanted to play ball, but that was clearly out of the question. When the games they'd brought with them were played out, Anna promoted ant races. It wasn't the greatest idea in the world: the ants kept straying and crossing paths. The children were at each other's throats by the fourth round, Jim's lip working as Sue taunted: "Crybaby, baby—"

"Why don't you throw her away!" he snarled.

It was the heat going to their heads. There'd been a bank of shade as wide as Anna was tall when they first came up, then a sash, then a ribbon, then nothing. The sun poured down. Suddenly Anna heard the sound of a dog straining at a leash. No dog up there.

It was Jim. "Ma—it's starting—" Anna didn't bother to ask what was starting. Jim blanched, his breath came with a battering sound. In-out, sharp as a hiccup.

She gathered him close. "Shhh. . ."

"I'm all tight, Ma. I'm gonna bust—I know it!"

"You're breathing now. You're doing an awful lot of

talking. If you couldn't breathe, you couldn't tell me how bad you feel," Anna said soothingly.

Sue kept her distance, a few yards off. "Is it his azz-mah?" She pronounced the name with respect.

"It'll be over soon, like it always is," Anna said firmly. "You sure don't help. Teasing like that."

The wheezing began, the long outward breaths.

When he began to cough, it was the easing sign. He reddened until the muck came up.

"There, that's better. I'm sure you feel better now," Anna insisted. Each cough gouged her a little.

Not long now, it would be time for lunch. And after lunch, nap time, blessed relief.

But Jim didn't want to lie down. By afternoon Anna was desperate. She wheedled the car keys away from Bob and drove to town in a burst of determination. The town was sultry, the main street all but deserted. What tourists there were visited the shops and restaurants only in the cool of the evening. Daytimes, the old men sat on benches in front of the band shell, chewing and spitting, staring into vacancy.

At the local soda hangout they divided a jubilee sundae three ways. Anna sat watching the local teenagers as they wasted time, no business more pressing than one another and the moment's sweetness. How normal, how comforting, the normal, she thought. The students at the Four Winds were from another planet.

She sat for a long while enjoying the cool, letting the children slop in the remains of the syrup and applying enough napkins to the table to stanch a wound. But cheerfully, cheerfully. And the children, sticky with chocolate, marshmallow and maraschino juice, seemed busy and content. She read the short menu over and over:

Bananafanna

45¢

Name your favorite dae:

The Night and Dae	Hot Fudge
The Good Old Dae	Hot Butterscotch
The Red Letter Dae	Strawberry Fruit
The Sunny Dae	Pineapple Fruit

Having spent a good deal more than she should have on this extravagance, Anna went completely overboard and treated the children to a round of miniature golf. She'd have to account for this sometime, but the reckoning was not yet.

They played nine holes and were way over par. Down the garden path—into the barn with the clapping door—scoot through the gap in the double wall—over the waterless moat and straight—twist through the labyrinth—sneak by the axe—past the pendulum of the tower clock—through the barrel of the cannon, smack—into the jaws of the lion: that obstacle course resembled nothing so closely as the emerging landscape of Anna's summer.

Later they bought some string licorice for after supper and walked out on the town landing to see the fishing boats come in. Now this is more like it, Anna thought. She even stopped to chat with the harbor master.

7

"CRUMBS," Aunt Ethel was saying as they
entered the dining room. They were late. The dish crew
was already clearing the table; Aunt Ethel was giving out
tips on how it should be done. "The secret of catching
crumbs—" She interrupted to warn Anna that lateness
meant an automatic penalty. If it happened again, they'd
simply have to make do without supper. "Here I am trying
to run a house for thirty people!" Thirty? The Homays
were four, the Elosons were two, there was Tertu, and
then the mynah bird—did he count? Add one for Larry,
in case. The students—how many? "This isn't a hotel, you
know." Anna knew.

What irritated Anna most of all was to see Bob sitting
there and nodding, saying nothing. Not quite saying nothing—his jaw bunched silently. But it wasn't enough to
grit your teeth and bear it, not nearly enough. She meant
to have it out with him later, for the umpteenth time. She
knew in advance that she'd get nowhere; it was all part of
his genius for avoiding conflict. Bob would do anything,

suffer any indignity, to keep the peace. "They won't sleep tonight," he'd say of the offenders, "but me—I'll sleep." Only it was Anna who usually lost sleep.

By eight-thirty Sue was so exhausted that she actually begged to be put to bed. But with Jim the memory of his asthma attack that morning was still too fresh. Although his head kept dropping—there'd be a little snap of his neck and he'd bolt awake—he wouldn't consent to close his eyes.

"Who's that big boy, the skinny one, the one with the bumps all over his face? You know, the one that talks so funny."

"Who do you mean?"

"You know, the one that's all creepy. He sticks by himself."

"I guess you mean Isaiah. He isn't creepy, Jim. He's just very smart. That makes him different from other people and a little lonesome. You shouldn't make fun of him."

"I don't care if he's smart, I don't like him. He's creepy. He's got a creepy name."

Bob was required to attend all the student lectures and there was something on embryology that evening. It was well after ten before he was free.

Anna smiled in greeting but, before she could get a word out, he forestalled her. "No discussions tonight, hon— Too tired, I'm whipped."

There never will be another time, Anna thought, not unless we have it out now. It will be one thing on top of another all summer long. What we need is some sort of strategy right from the start. If we could take an attitude and stick to it, at least for the sake of our self-respect— can't he see that? Maybe once he's changed his clothes.

But Jim insisted he'd only go to bed if his daddy took him. Then that wasn't enough: he wanted a story.

"No more stories!" Anna declared from the next room. "You've had one already."

"That one was out of a book. I want a real story."

"Close your eyes, kipper," Bob said, "I'll think of something."

"That's appeasement, Bob. It's funny—" Anna couldn't help interrupting, and with some anger, "you have all the time in the world for stories, but not a minute to spare for the facts of our life here—"

She was going to say more when Jim broke in with a quick succession of coughs, five little counterfeits.

"You two competing?" Bob asked wearily.

"Go ahead, Bob," Anna gave in as she always did. "Will you at least try and make it snappy?"

Bob began an endless tale about a salesman on a train from West Virginia.

When it was all over, he staggered into the next room. "So help me, God—" he said.

"Didn't know you had it in you," Anna hailed him. "You nearly put *me* to sleep. That was the silliest performance."

"Am I ever bushed," Bob sighed, groping for his pajamas in the dark. "No, don't bother—I don't need it." He was too tired to turn on a lamp. "Grin and bear it," he said, lifting the blanket, "that's my philosophy."

"Look the other way and maybe the problem will go away—that's also your philosophy," Anna couldn't help adding. "Don't you want to talk about this afternoon?"

"Do I?" he muttered. "Anna, what's the use?"

"Look, Bob, suppose you were standing in a bog of quicksand, wouldn't you want to know? To know and to fight it? Even if all your struggles to pull clear of it were bound to fail, wouldn't you at least want to know?"

"Not really. No, I wouldn't want to know. Not if there were nothing I could do about it. I'd rather go down smiling. Besides—you're being silly."

"But I'm serious."

"Then there isn't an ounce of logic in your head, Anna. Where's your sense of proportion? Hm? Where's this bog of quicksand? I don't see anything resembling it at the Four Winds. As usual, you're exaggerating. Dramatizing everything. You're disappointed, that's understandable. It isn't quite the summer we planned. It so happens we made a mistake, we're counselors at what turns out to be the wrong camp. A mistake—big deal! It's no bed of roses here, but that doesn't make it a bog of quicksand. You go from one extreme to the other. Life isn't a bed of roses, Anna. Marriage isn't a bed of roses. Grow up. You're making something out of nothing. One of life's small letdowns. And now, if you don't mind, I'd like some sleep."

On that note of sound and sober sense, Bob Homay turned over on his side. And was at once asleep: unanswerable.

8

ONE BY ONE, lights went out in the Four Winds. First the students', then the Homays'. Chief next. He went up to bed without looking in on his wife. No use telling her not to sit up late; he'd tried that before and she rewarded him with silence and one of those you-ruined-my-life looks. Waste of breath even saying goodnight.

Tertu was the last to stumble up to bed. Aunt Ethel sat on alone in the small dining room. She was in a state of comfortable "undress"—flannel nightgown, woolen bathrobe and a blanket thrown like a sarape over her shoulders.

She'd been writing out menus for the coming week. They'd have potatoes and salt-pork gravy seven days out of seven, if it was left up to Tertu. Or corned hake, that was her idea of a big treat. If the students had their way, it would be nothing but éclairs, pizza and pickles. It was up to Aunt Ethel to make sure their diet was properly balanced.

Even with all her wrappings and the windows fast, it was cold. Her hands were ice. Bed would have been cozier, but Aunt Ethel was wide awake. So she sat on, nursing a cup of cocoa and a cigarette. Now and then she glanced up at the cage in the corner. Larry was being mighty quiet, had been for days.

"You awake, love? Anything wrong?"

"Whoopee!" said Larry.

"This is my last cigarette."

Larry cocked his head with a certain skepticism.

"I could chew gum instead, but it always ends up tasting like rubber bands. Say, how does this sound—fish chowder, macaroni and cheese, coleslaw and cobbler, hm? Too starchy, you think?"

"What you doin'?" said Larry.

"So many details . . ." Aunt Ethel sighed. "A million and one things to do, a million and one things to look after. And who will look after them if I don't? I'd like to know."

"What you doin'?" said Larry.

"Nothin' much," she answered, "not even smoking." Her cigarette was about to tip backwards from the rim of her saucer. She flicked off the column of ash and took a deep drag on a very short butt. It was so perfectly still she could hear the ash flake and fall. "Nothing at all," she confessed, "sitting here by my lonesome. Can't sleep, Larry, don't know why. It's no use trying. I just begin to come alive when the sun goes down.

"Hear that?" She paused. A sound like steps. She coughed a few times, by way of query. There was no answering sound, except for the wind banging the wheelbarrow against the shed. "Have to speak to Alfred about that tomorrow. Remind me to catch him before he leaves."

"Night's a very busy time, you know. People don't seem to realize. Most of us are born and die sometime between three and four in the morning. That's a fact. Somebody ought to find out why. Maybe you know. Hm? C'mon, Lar, I want an opinion, any kind of opinion—anything. What's the matter with you lately? Why the silent treatment?"

Testing, she thought, he's testing me.

"All right, if that's the way you're going to be. Since you have nothing to say for yourself, I'm going to call a blackout. Yes, I am. You don't think I'm going to do it, do you? I've got the cover in my hand."

She counted to sixty-five, then lowered the hood. The instant darkness came over him, Larry began to squawk. Aunt Ethel lifted the cover halfway. "You see!" she said triumphantly. "See how you like that? Well, that's what silence is to me."

"Good morning Larry," said Larry.

"So I give up," she conceded, lifting the cover entirely. She detached the cage from the stand and set it down on the table in front of her. She was used to taking Larry from room to room with her in this way, a bad habit of treating the cage with the bird in it as she would a potted plant. Some people talked to plants, though she wouldn't.

Alfred did, she'd overheard him talking to the young shoots of corn. Or maybe singing without a tune. She couldn't make out what the words were.

She withdrew a fresh cigarette, tamped it twice, then let it drop from her fingers, let her hands fall to the table. There wasn't a sound now. The house might have been empty, nothing stirred.

There was so little gaiety in the household. Summer after summer, she had seen it happen. There was industry, even excellence, but no joy.

Was this really so? Or did happiness evaporate in her presence, fly off at her approach? It was as if she cast a long shadow wherever she went. And crossing the lawn, as she did each evening after supper, the grass seemed gray and the leaves gray. Lately it seemed to her that twilight was becoming her permanent time.

The wires creaked. She looked up gratefully. Larry hopped to his perch. "You alive or dead?" she challenged. "C'mon Larry, don't spite me.

"There's nobody to talk to here, have you noticed? Anna's like a mother hen, full of her chicks. Tertu treats words like dollars and cents, she doesn't waste any. With Alfred it's nothing but whether the slugs are biting, whether to mulch or not to mulch. And Frank's the worst of all. Busy, busy, all the time. Busy avoiding, I say. No time for anything but his perfusion circuits, **his** heart vents and bypasses, laser-light knives—and whatnots.

"Let's not forget the whatnots, Larry. He's never been an idle man. Let's see . . . First there was Lenore. Lenore with the beautiful voice.

"I had a beautiful voice, myself. Frank said so. He said:

'Ethel, you ought to go on the stage.' We were courting then—he'd have said anything."

She'd always had a small voice, inclined to shrillness when she tried to project. Still, there'd been a certain sweetness in it.

No voice left, in any case. Smoking had taken care of that. She'd taken up smoking in earnest about the same time that Frank had taken up with Marsha. Or was it with the next girl?

Who *was* the next girl? There was a Frances somewhere along the line. Frances before Marsha? Marsha came before Robin, she was clear on that at least. Both those girls strung him along. His forty-third birthday and wasn't it predictable? Talk about menopausal women! There'd been a new girl every few months after Robin. She'd lost track until he started up with Fern.

"*That*, my friend, was a serious business. That mattered. I don't believe anything happened. It was just about to happen when I stepped in. But he's still hankering after her, I can tell. Daydreams about her. All the time. Anyhow, the affair is over. Fern's gone. Hasn't touched me since—is that fair, Larry? Punishing me because *he* played around and got burnt? You figure that one out.

"C'mon, talk to me, Larry. Nobody but you and me in this big old house. Nobody to talk to. What do you think of it up here?

"Do you think at all?" And, poking her fingers through the wires, coaxing with the tip of her little finger as though it were something very good to eat, she added: "Penny for your thoughts . . ."

9

SUNDAY. A day little different from other days of the week at Spemann Lab. In spite of the fact that they were only a mile from the Four Winds, and members of a parent organization, the Spemann staff had yet to meet the students. A staff conference had been scheduled for three-thirty that afternoon to decide who would sponsor what; they were late this year and immediate action was necessary.

Drs. Burton and Kamin met in the hallway leading to the director's office. Burton kept his eye fixed on the door. A modest door, with a panel of frosted glass reading: A. ALKAVIST—COME IN. It was locked. They were early, the others had not yet arrived. Burton paced in silence for a while. Kamin sat on the long bench—the petitioners' bench, as the junior staff liked to call it. Two metal canes rested against his knees. He was chewing on an uncut cigar, which he never bothered to light, and casting a disgruntled eye on the display case in the middle of the corridor.

It was a large glass cylinder featuring an intricate piece of sculpture. From a distance the structure was unintelligible. From closer up, and with the aid of a copious legend, it became a clear, if craftsy, representation of a fraction of a DNA molecule. A home job. Dr. Alkavist had strung it together with Duco cement, using dime-store marbles for the atoms of the nucleotides—blue for adenine, yellow for thymine, black for guanine, cytosine crystalline clear—linking them together with pipe cleaners for the purine and pyrimidine rungs and the sugar-phosphate uprights. He'd labeled it dramatically: THE FOUNDATION OF LIFE.

"What is this mishegass?" Kamin waved his cigar ambiguously.

"What's 'misegosh'?"

"This sponsorship business. How'd we get into this thing?"

"One of the privileges of working at Spemann. You must have known, Sid. This place is famous for it, Alkavist's pet project, Operation Youth. Or should I say, in keeping with the old man's operatic style, Operation Sunrise?" Burton smiled broadly as he spoke. He'd learned to take life as it came: pretty various.

Besides, it was hard for Burton to see the bleak side of things this fine day. It had been a week of fine days. Yesterday he'd paid off the mortgage on his house. And today he was wearing his favorite shirt, flamingo pink dashed with vivid green palm fronds, a souvenir from the

Bahamas. The shirt both reflected and further colored his mood—a vivifying cycle. Sid took everything far too seriously—self-righteously, even. He'd have himself a coronary before hitting fifty if he didn't watch it.

Sidney Kamin was relatively young, in his late thirties, and already in possession of a secure reputation in his field, one that would have satisfied many an older man. Yet he worked like someone who had done nothing yet and was under the verdict of time; he worked like a man with only a year to live. It wasn't his health. Aside from his paralysis, long since surmounted, he had no ailments. He made his way swiftly on two canes, shifting his weight by means of his powerful arms.

His response to Burton was typical: "You know, of course, that I gave up a cushy university post, a chair with a swank title, just to be free of this kind of trap. Committee work, student conferences, these things eat up hours and days. But, even there, I never wasted an hour with college students. They were pre-doctoral level before they got to waste my time. And now I'm supposed to take on high-school students—teenagers! It's a bad joke."

"C'mon, Sid, one student is all you're required. How much disruption can one student create? You have to understand—this is Alkavist's dream. Think of it his way for a change. He's getting on. He wants to develop the future faster; there are some things he'd like to see licked in his time. That's understandable, isn't it? The younger they are, the more open they are. These are the formative years."

"You're mistaken there. The years one to five—they're

the formative ones. If he's looking for raw material, stuff that's really malleable."

"He can't very well snatch from the cradle, Sid."

None of this succeeded in mollifying Kamin, who muttered, "Give up my time—to kids? Not my own kids. I resent it, Henry. Can't say how much I resent it."

"You've got options. I envy you: you can pick and choose. Go elsewhere if one kid is going to put you out. Otherwise, live with it—relax. These kids don't eat up all that much time. And they're so grateful, they really are. They're awfully sweet, most of them, and they're—you know . . . inner-directed. They are. They need very little —a few kind words, some advice, a tip from a seasoned professional, a scrap of equipment on loan, a couple of hours a week, and they're thrilled. Come on, Sid, admit it—don't you want to play God?"

Kamin clamped down on his cigar but said nothing.

There were voices on the floor below, a guide's, level and clear, verses, antiphons, responsories. "Oooh, the itsy bitsies!" one voice crescendoed above the rest. Kamin winced. Evidently a tour was in progress. The group must have reached the display mice in the vestibule.

Burton had the feeling he was pacifying a child. "Cheer up," he consoled, "choose the likeliest. I was on the final selection committee. Some of those kids look damn promising—no joke. There's one from Brooklyn—I've seen his résumé. It's pretty impressive. Interests a little scattered, all over the map, I'll admit. But he did some work on his own with seizure thresholds in mice. Doesn't sound like a time-waster to me."

65

"What's his name?"

"Now you've got me. Name? Something a little grandiose—Jeremiah? Name like that. Last name begins with a 'Y'—Yellowitz? Now I'm guessing. How many names begin with 'Y'? And how many kids can there be from Brooklyn?"

"Seizure thresholds, you're sure? Last name begins with a 'Y'? All right, if it has to be, let it be him. I'll take him on your say-so. Let me have the first bid, will you?"

"Sure. Sam usually takes on any kid who uses the phrase 'tumor transplant' in his project proposal. It's that easy for him. He feels he has nothing to lose. Believe me, it's that simple. Treat their projects as warm-up exercises and you'll never miss. You might even be pleasantly surprised."

"I very much doubt it," said Kamin.

10

On July 5th, the names of the sponsors were given out. It promised to be a very good summer for tumor and organ transplants and immunological studies. Sponsors had been found for every proposal but one. Only Stevie Conroy was going ahead on a project without supervision: a comparison of alternative bedding materials for mice. The students teased him about it; they considered it a silly investigation; at the same time, they all realized that the commercial possibilities of a new material would be sizable.

A few pet schemes were modified, but none was abandoned. Some of the students with interests that were close or overlapping had teamed up at the last moment and made joint proposals. Polly and Naomi would be working together on the feeding patterns of obese mice. Dr. Burton had a three-day symposium in Trieste, so it would be at least another week until they sat down to discuss details with him.

Naomi would be working alone with Dr. Lebret on a tissue-culture project—epithelium of mouse ear. So far, she'd only met Lebret once, a big fellow with callused hands and the high color of a deep-sea fisherman. Although he didn't look it, he was a world authority in his field. Naomi had discovered his *Fundamentals of Cell Culture* only that year. She'd found it breathtaking—the idea of keeping cells alive outside the body seemed to hold a promise of eluding death—and she had begun to idolize the author from a long distance. And now here she was!

It amazed everyone to learn that Isaiah, the rugged individualist, was sharing a project with Joel—a study of audiogenic seizures in mice. "The effect of 'The Blue Danube' on waltzing mice," Isaiah called it in one of his rare light moments. In reality, the music was a doorbell and a washbasin; the "waltz" looked like an epileptic fit, and often turned out to be a dance of death.

Their sponsor was Dr. Kamin, a newcomer to Spemann Lab. He had a certain reputation for speed and rigor; his interest was in pure research, he left practical applications to others. He had a very low tolerance for distraction, shunned teaching and the writing of textbooks; he was distinguished enough to be able to do this. So it came as a complete surprise to learn that Kamin had agreed to take on, not one, but *two* student projects. There was no accounting for it: one project per sponsor was the norm.

Kamin had taken on Isaiah's second project, a study of the effects of anoxia on the brain, an interest which none of the other students could even begin to share.

The students' labs at the Four Winds were in a series

of small rooms on the upper story, converted from what must have been servants' rooms or storage nooks. They were on the same level as the Homays so, for the first time, Naomi realized what the Homays must have been suffering in the heat of the afternoon. The rooms were stifling and so low it was impossible to stand upright where the eaves sloped. Each had a small dormer window which did not permit much air. Naomi shared a lab with Polly; Joel and Isaiah were next door.

Twice a week, the students were scheduled to go over to Spemann, confer with their sponsors, and discuss difficulties.

Sunday evenings Dr. Alkavist gave special lectures. "Just talks," he called them. They weren't technical, so everyone in the house was encouraged to attend, including Tertu, who only came for the first and then stood in the doorway shaking her head quietly for three or four minutes before she walked off.

Half an hour before the lecture was scheduled, the students would set up the common room, open up the folding chairs and make sure the lectern was appointed with water pitcher and glass. The talk was inspirational, or tried to be. Bread-and-butter lectures were held during the week; these took place in the seminar room, where the blackboard had prominence.

Sundays, the Alkahest would take the lectern and turn it into a pulpit. It was a sort of preachy prose poetry, a kind of song. He rarely gave them cases or examples, nothing but sweeping generalization, flourish upon flourish. His optimism, meliorism, rampant rationalism would be unthinkable ten years later. But even at the time, he was not *of* the time; his view of the human prospect had gone beyond Darwinism into some dream of infinite perfectability that was nothing if not religious. In the stern clarity of her fifteen years and two weeks, Naomi decided he must have lost his wits when he became head of Spemann. Or maybe the other way round: he became an administrator when people began to suspect he was losing his marbles. Kicked upstairs; it happened. He was really old, with hair all gone white and a vein standing out on his left temple. Sometimes his voice would fray, an old man's voice.

"If science isn't the hope of the future, the hope of the world, the only cure for war, the best cure for social ills, then what is? What is? Whatever is?" He paused, but not long enough for anyone in the audience to come up with an alternative. "Mystery? Miracle? Authority?" Lifting his arms, he supplied the options.

"Where have any of these gotten us?" Some of the students looked down at their shoes: not far, clearly. "Problems will be solved with intelligence," he said, "or they won't be solved at all.

"Is the nuclear family the best form of social organization? Is genetic engineering an evil? How can we know unless we find out? How can we find out? By prayer, incantation and fasting? Should we toss a coin? Read tea leaves? Palms? Stars? Consult the local guru or the entrails of a goat?

"How can we decide what's best for men? There is a method and you know that method. A method of patient observation and endless, unremitting self-correction. A method of conditions and consequences, of temporary answers to provisional questions. It offers nothing infallible and nothing final—no absolutes, no wholesale solutions. Its weakness is its strength. It is our only hope, our only way of achieving that unity of theory and practice without which we are half-human, spinners of words, of airy nothings, or muddlers—wasters of the earth and despoilers of life."

Naomi was sitting next to Jerome Marten, who kept kicking her chair leg, swift little kicks in a broken rhythm. She kept trying to catch his eye to tell him to cut it out, but he was staring resolutely at a point on the wall above the speaker. His face had a stony set. There'd been quite a disturbance when Jerome asked to be excused early from dish crew so as to make it to Mass on Sunday. His request was treated as some sort of apostasy. He was either Catholic or Episcopalian, the high kind, and Naomi was amazed to hear him asking to go to church of his own volition, nobody forcing him. The pressures were all the other way.

"Consider Prometheus," the Alkahest went on. "The scientific way is what Charles Morris has called 'the Promethean Way.'"

No one knew who Charles Morris was, but the students, in their several fashions, all considered Prometheus. Naomi thought of his gift of fire, Jerome of his chains and the predatory birds.

"In Prometheus stealing fire from the gods to give to man we have a picture of the Scientist, the Technologist, the World Shaper."

Hans started a list; he passed it to his neighbor, who passed it on. By the time it came round to Naomi, it read:

Fire/Wheel/Lever/Plow
Catapult/Cosmetics
Gunpowder/Aspirin
Anesthetics
Auschwitz/Muzak/Penicillin

Each line was in a different hand.

Naomi wrote: Pulley/Zipper. Then she added: Movable type/DDT.

Jerome printed carefully: Cooking/Contraception/Insurance/Hiroshima. The list stalled with him. He was listening intently to the Alkahest.

"If anything is to blame for the moral defeatism of modern times, I have to point a finger at religion. Sad, but true. The great religions of the world have tried, I'll grant that much. At best, they've been sincere but premature attempts to grapple with the unknown. But they've been monopolistic in their claims to truth. And divisive—setting man against man. The great religions have accounted for their full share of man's inhumanity to man. Let's face it—they've had their chance"

"Religious faith has had thousands of years to transform the earth and the quality of human life, and with what results? You tell me." He lifted his glass, sipped, set it down. Waited.

Not a sound.

"Bankrupt," the Alkahest pronounced. "Bankrupt."

"Who's tried? How many?" said Jerome in a very small voice.

Anna Homay, seated on Jerome's right, looked up, blinked briefly, cast a puzzled glance at Jerome, then at the Alkahest, then looked down again at the rings on her left hand. She sat there, slowly turning her rings, a ritual Naomi had witnessed a hundred times before. Married women were always studying their rings. Naomi wondered what the gesture meant. Was she slyly flaunting her wealth? Or reconsidering the bargain?

"The fire of faith will illuminate a secular, Promethean religion *because of its risks*, because of adventure, because it does not promise pie in the sky. Most people don't realize how young science is. Only a few centuries. Give it a chance. The attempt to focus the methods of science on human problems is only beginning. To give up the struggle this early, as so many young people nowadays are doing, is to abdicate. To abdicate your birthright as human beings.

"Don't do it," the Alkahest appealed to them. "I know you won't give up. Unless youth and adventure are really dead—and I have only to look around me at your young and eager faces to deny this with my whole heart—such surrender to unreason can only be viewed as self-mutilation or suicide. Truth is the only goal for men who are free."

And, yes, there was something more. Naomi didn't remember how he led up to it or how it tied in, but this one detail impressed her. Maybe because it was so refreshingly concrete. He said that when Sigmund Freud was a young medical student, he wrote a significant histological

73

paper for which he dissected four hundred eels. Freud went to the trouble of dissecting four hundred eels to make sure his conclusions were founded on fact. Did anyone appreciate how difficult it was to dissect an eel?

None of the students did. Naomi considered her single earthworm, then felt ashamed.

"Four hundred eels!" the Alkahest intoned. "And that was the measure of the man lost to science when he turned to other things."

He ended on a note of benediction, spreading his arms wide. "The Four Winds is not just a house. It is a new beginning, a test case. We are gathered here to form a community of shared intelligence and purpose, committed to the methods of science, devoted to progress and love of work. Work—work hard and well. And may this be the shining hour in your lives. When everything is possible and nothing forfeit to what has gone before."

After the Alkahest left, the students gathered in the kitchen for snacks.

"What did you think of the sermon?" Joel met Naomi over a warm loaf of banana cake.

"Think of it—eels!" said Naomi, still impressed. "Four hundred of them!"

"You're cute," said Joel, very quick. He backed off without waiting for a response. But couldn't help grinning. "Hey, Leo, are you cutting that cake or defending it?" he sang out.

11

SOCIAL HOUR, snack time . . . everything according to a fixed schedule. By ten-thirty or, at the very latest, a quarter to eleven, lights went out in the students' quarters. Three times a week at bedtime Aunt Ethel made the rounds with two bottles, one with milk of magnesia, the other with Kaopectate, to make sure everyone was on track.

Vito, Johnny and Jerome talked after lights went out. About girls mainly—"real girls," the likes of which they wouldn't see again until fall. Jerome, who went to an all-boys boarding school and who kept company with the scholars, not the jocks, had nothing to contribute to these discussions. He had no girl of his own; the closest he had ever come was a silent, hopeless crush on his roommate's younger sister. So he listened to Vito and Johnny, kept them going with apt questions, waiting, only waiting for the privacy that would be his when they subsided, somewhere short of midnight.

Jerome had little use for chatter, He wanted desperately to open up and talk, really talk to someone. Since that wasn't possible, he preferred silence.

Writing letters did not ease him. He wrote letters to his parents, but those were formalities only; he never told them what he thought. For his parents, Jerome had a twisted but fierce affection; he felt it was up to him to protect them from the shattering facts of life. They were so young still, so unsullied. They married after graduating from high school, having known each other all their lives, and Jerome had spent his first years in an enchanted space. His home was an imitation English manor house, set off by velvet lawns, in the town's most gracious section. Jerome was convinced that living behind mullioned windows, viewing the world as a mosaic trimmed to the measure of those grids, had a profound cloistering effect. He had moved on, but his parents still lived behind them.

With his parents, Jerome had made a disruptive third. "Too bright for us to handle" was how they explained sending him off to boarding school at the age of seven.

Jerome's version differed: "No room for anyone else, full of each other." He'd said that in a bitter moment, remembering how long he'd been away at boarding school, feeling he'd been born an old man. "They left me to be my own parents."

He kept a journal and gave himself advice. When he was at school, he kept his journal with his notebooks; it was a spiral notebook, no different from the others; he was able to delve into it any time he pleased without attracting the slightest attention. Often he jotted down a note in the middle of class, the moment it occurred to him, no one the wiser.

No chance of that at the Four Winds. Here every action was subjected to the most public scrutiny, everyone kept in line, doing more or less similar things at the same time. And yet Jerome *had* to write, in the same way Johnny and Vito had to talk, if only to cast a shadow, to make sure that he was there at all. He'd bought two flashlights in Boston: one was a country lantern with a flicker-or-flash option; the other was a tiny thing on a key chain, smaller than a pen. He could try writing under the covers with it, the light was only a pinpoint, but even that was enough to attract notice—he'd tried it before. Vito and Johnny would be sure to tease him about it if they found out. Only girls kept diaries.

The bathroom! That made sense. Jerome extricated one foot. The air, the floor, were arctic. It was crazy, the trouble he was taking for this notebook In the morning he'd be tired and regret it.

A buoy rang out, he could hear it, a hoarse, cold note, as if coming from deep down under. The sea made a dragging sound.

The notebook was under his mattress. Slide, don't lift— Throwing his extra blanket around his shoulders, Jerome filed quietly past the sleepers.

First sleep was deepest, he was counting on that. He eased the door shut. No sound, except for the click as he released the knob. Anything? No. He settled in.

The light was scant enough. The silence . . . but it wasn't really that quiet. There was the muffled coughing

77

of drains and then, briefly, voices in the pipes, the tail end
of a quarrel. "You can go to hell!" the high voice said.
"Isn't this it?" said the bass. A door slammed. Curious.
He thought he recognized the voices, he wasn't sure. The
pipes were a distorting factor. It was cold, even his ball-
point pen was cold. He drew it twice across the empty
page before the ink would come. Then he began to
scrawl:

July 10
Four Winds

There was somebody awake a moment ago, two somebodies.
I heard voices. Was it the Elosons? Now there's nothing doing.
Only a little night music—the drains keep humming. Here I
am, seated on the can and fondling my little pen. I've got this
pressing need.

What can I say about the Four Winds? A few things stand
out. Like Chief and Aunt Ethel. They're both chain-smokers.
Sometimes they don't even bother to touch their lips. Which
makes me think they smoke for the sake of the ritual itself,
they have a need for ritual and it's not a question of taste or
touch or any other thing.

The Homays. A complete family hidden away upstairs. I
could do with a little privacy myself. The only privacy I get
is like now, well after midnight.

The girls here really aren't much (except for one) and I'm
no connoisseur. There's a skinny one. She's intensely cross-
eyed. Jen-ise from Jaw-ja. Another—Polly. Fat but very nice,
no nonsense. Then there's Naomi, a Brooklyn girl. She's
scruffy and built like an eleven-year-old. The only thing I can
say in her favor is that she has dimples. She's so awfully
positive. And is she really? I scared her half to death when I

had to take blood from her arm. I scared myself—my hands were shaking.

Then there's Eva. She's more than pretty. How does *she* fit in? Don't ask. Be grateful.

I mean to get to the roof one of these days. The view must be terrific. The roof doesn't come to a true peak but levels out. There's a captain's walk with a white railing up there, so it's meant to be walked on. I don't plan to ask permission. Just seize the hour.

I've been trying to piece the history of the Four Winds together with only a few facts to go on. The house belonged to Dr. Alkavist. (I call him the Alkahest. The name's caught on with the other students. Out of his hearing, of course. It must fit.)

The house really belonged to his wife. It was bequeathed to the Alkahest. His wife died very young, of leukemia apparently, a family disease on the mother's line. They had no kids. Her family had money. In Rhine wines or something like that—I'm not sure. Out of these few poor facts I weave a romance, a regular soap opera.

The family was very posh—the Four Winds was only one of several summer establishments, each complete with servants' quarters and gatehouse (ours are now Rabbit House and Mouse House, respectively). The Four Winds was left to the Alkahest, who chose never to live in it.

The house was completely stripped down. Whether the Alkahest did this or his wife's family, I don't know. Furniture, fixtures, paintings—not a signature on the premises. Only one trace left as far as I've discovered. It's in the small dining room where the Elosons eat. I found out when I was assigned to dish crew and went in to clear the table. Over the buffet was a large oil portrait in an ornate frame.

It's a woman's portrait. The wife? I'm only guessing. I like

79

to think that's who it was. I like to think she explains it, the Alkahest's monomania, his unremitting fidelity. (He never remarried, he's still working on leukemia.)

First glance—there's nothing remarkable. A fashionable woman with understated features. (The best schools, riding lessons, the works.) Pale lips. Quiet hair. A background of heavy comfort—a wall of books bound in calf, brocade curtain, leather armchair. I looked again and was only impressed by the woman's ornaments, a single strand of pearls and a jade ring—these, full of light and color, lovingly rendered. The woman is wearing a soft green blouse. It is loose with only the haziest suggestion of breasts. The sleeves are pushed up to the elbows. One arm lies on the armrest, the hand droops forward, dragging the eye down. That hand is huge and gravid, insupportable, too heavy to lift or bear. The ring is heavy on the middle finger, the fingers are heavy. Two forking veins heave and swell over the metacarpal bones.

The other arm is half raised, balanced on the point of the elbow. It is small and flirtatious, light as a feather, the wrist cunningly turned, the fingers teasing the chin.

I keep coming back to the face. The cheeks and lips have a midnight pallor. There are blue moons under the eyes. And the eyes themselves are clear and gray. Something about those eyes— They have that far-off look you see in the portraits of great men. No time for the middle distance, say those eyes, no time for the near—we are fastened on the Far.

Terrible—it's a terrible painting except for those eyes.

When his wife died, the Alkahest was an associate staff member working on the question of the inheritability of a predisposition to leukemia. He developed a strain of mice with 90% incidence by brother-sister matings over twenty generations—*that* pure. The Four Winds was used as a guest-house for visiting scientists working in many loosely related fields believed to have some bearing on "cancer research"—whatever that may be. We're told that there are only neoplastic diseases, more or less similar and different. Quite possibly as broad and various a grouping as infectious diseases. So "cancer" may be no more useful a term than "infection." It says precious little specific by itself.

Herb Smith filled me in with something interesting. At some point (I don't know when), the Alkahest took a post as president of a large midwestern university, not a fly-by-night, but some very solid institution. Herb wouldn't identify it except to say that it was someplace long established, with a good name. But the assignment didn't last long. The Alkahest turned out to be too progressive for the progressives, too utopian even for the utopians. His budget was slanted to the experimental programs rather than the established curriculum. And he favored the science faculties at the expense of liberal arts. So of course he made many enemies.

So— He returned to Spemann and began to think of education outside the university, apprenticeships and internships. He thought if he could train the coming generation well enough in advance, there'd be no time lost, no transmission gap. He began with college students, no problem, and then went on to set up a younger group. I guess his thinking went like this: Suppose one of these students began working on anything—say, leukemia. Say he began sharpening his focus at age sixteen. With an early start, that would mean a gain of some ten years. Out of a hundred students, ten might continue—a cumulative saving of a hundred years! Not to mention fifteen others working in related fields and some twenty or thirty working in fields apparently unrelated or only loosely related. A breakthrough in one area might have repercussions in all. On hopes like these, the summer program was founded and the Four Winds given over entirely to the students. A group of educators, interested in early career prediction and "tracking" of students, came in with funds and surveys.

So here we are. We are charged with a great commission. About us the hopes of the nation hover—for isn't science the hope of the nation? Of the world? And here I am. Whatever my doubts—it's a fact—I'm here among the chosen.

Then why can't I sleep properly? I've been sleeping fitfully, in snatches. I had an awful dream. I was at dissection. The animal was a man and lay open on a board. All the organs were spilled out on the ground like pieces of a jigsaw puzzle. I had to put them back in the right places. I did it, all but two—the heart, I think, and something else unrecognizable that kept changing its color and shape and slipping out of my hands. The trouble was that it had no angles or defined edges. I tried, twisting and twisting, but the two pieces wouldn't go back. A sense of urgent time pressure. I was in an ampitheater in a pit, and above me were rows and rows of faces looking down. Riboldi—my sponsor. And Chief. Eva waved and called out—Hey, Jerome! Leo and Hans were there, Vito and Johnny, the Homay kids, someone in a green smock and lots of people I didn't recognize. They were all looking down at me. A man shouted: "Lookit that! The Assistant Professor of Pastrami!"

And I woke up in a sweat.

This evening the Alkahest delivered his weekly sermon. Text: *Science, the Hope of the World*. If our hearts were pure that might be true. But since they aren't . . .

He said something strange about four hundred eels.

Consider Prometheus, he said. I did. A curious choice of emblem, I thought. After all, who was Prometheus? A bungler with kindest intentions. A pirate who stole what he could not create. And then again, consider fire. For this gift, mixed thanks.

What else? A plea for proper pride. Man the master, lord of the food chain. Eats all and is eaten by none.

The muchness and suchness of the times. Or words to that effect.

Science would prevail would prevail would prevail would— Nothing wholesale, nothing absolute—but science would cure all ills. Curiouser and curiouser.

And words about nothing forfeit to what has gone before. A halcyon age, a shining hour. But again, that's not true. Everything is forfeit, though not entirely. We carry all of history on our backs, human history and all the patterns of life that have gone before. Look at the human fetus—but he knows this.

It's all a song of consolation, whistling in the dark, nothing more. A well-meaning man, a spinner of tales and nostrums, our Alkahest.

I wish I could stop mulling and mulling over things and sleep soundly for once. To be secure in a tight little pellicle of cellulose or something—

It's so late and I'm so tired.

12

JULY 11TH. An hour before sunup. The house: rocking a little in the swells, except for the nocturnal mice, all its passengers floating free. Even Aunt Ethel slept. She lay on her heart side, her left arm crumpled under her ribs. In a moment she would shift sides. Her sleep was at its deepest. She did not even dream.

Then she reversed, swinging her full weight. Chief made a strangled sound, reached out, snatched a handful of air, grappling to hold on to his interrupted dream. He fumbled, lost his hold, struggled to find another entry— by what orifice—hatch—window—door? Try as he might, the blue hills of his vision had sunk beneath the surface of the lake and he could not again raise them. A vision of purity and peace, a single motion had shattered it.

Aunt Ethel shifted again, back to starting position, then lay still. Chief fell off into a light doze. He was standing on a pier, leaning on a spiked fence, watching the girl pass by. First a yacht—not a soul aboard, going at a clip. Behind it, a girl in a tagboat was hallooing and waving—at him! Her hair was sunny. He stood motionless. He wanted to make a sign in return but he noticed his hands were fixed to the fence, his palms impaled. The girl's voice grew fainter, the water widening between them. The light, the light in her hair dazzled his eyes, his ears were ringing. He woke—his heart bolting—dizzy for chase—

Woke to a darkness.

And fell off again. He found himself being packed into a brown paper bag. The bag said "Bohack!" speaking its name quite clearly. Chief said nothing. His wife carried him home from the supermarket with the rest of the groceries. He was in with the meats. After she entered the house, she put the bag down on the kitchen table and opened the refrigerator, then the frozen-food compartment. She reached for him—

—the cold reached him, woke him. Somehow he had rolled free of his blankets. It was quiet in the house and beyond.

In the dim light, he studied the torso of his wife, humped buttocks and back, a boulder, ready to roll and flatten him. There was no air. He couldn't endure his bed a minute longer, nor could he abide the closeness of his wife's body. The blankets, whose warmth he had savored, stifled him now. He wanted to flee the house, his wife, himself. He longed to press his face upon the breathing earth. Was it his heart? Would dying be like this?

The first light defined the window, the first birds began.

He got up, touched the floor with a shock, and tiptoed

to the lavatory. He closed the door carefully behind him.

Sad business. All that tumescence for such meager drops? He studied the situation gravely: the word for it was "stricture," but the word didn't say much. Rain of the idle grape, rain of the withered vine . . . that was more like it. He leaned lightly against the wall, pressing his cheek to the tile. It was silky and cool. The contact soothed him, and he lingered there for some minutes, thinking of nothing at all. Then he returned to his wife's side.

Not long after, Aunt Ethel woke with a start. She'd heard something, some alarm. What? It wasn't the usual three gongs but something else. A fiddle, she was sure of it. How could that be? A country fiddle, whining and scraping. How many fiddlers were there on the premises?

The tides were next, someone calling the tides: high tide, low tide, coastal warnings. Tertu's radio—of course!

Larry's cage stood in a dark corner, hooded, silent. The fringes of the cover swayed softly. He must have been awake and stirring within. Aunt Ethel watched the fringes move and did nothing. She wasn't in the least bit eager to lift the cover and greet Larry these days. He hadn't said a word to her in more than a week; she'd coaxed and coaxed, but he'd only tilted his head and eyed her dully, without a spark of recognition. She knew it was ridiculous, but she couldn't help feeling he was doing it to spite her, using the same tactics her husband did—silence and absence.

Chief and Larry—they were both most infuriatingly there and not there.

She turned to Chief and studied his face in slumber. A vein in his temple pulsed softly. It was some time before she realized that he was completely awake, buying time by shamming sleep. She could tell from his breathing and the tension of his mouth. Anything to avoid a conversation. Let him lie then, dreaming no doubt of the perfused liver, the perfused heart, the reinforced omentum. Lips bunched like a fig—blotto position. His eyelids were modestly shut, but they sat on his face like doilies over luminous stains. His face was very red.

Chief was indeed wide awake, awake and dreaming his favorite waking dream, dissolving with joy behind his pallid lids.

The girl had changed from week to week in years past, but in his late age he'd fixed on one. Fern. Her name was Fern. She'd been his last girl and their affair had been the longest, the most unconsummated, the most devastating of all. Other affairs had come quickly to fruition (He "only fooled around," he warned them in advance.) Quickly bloomed and quickly withered away. This one never bloomed, it haunted and haunted him. "Unfinished-task effect"—the brokenness—it was a known phenomenon. Ethel had managed to get him up to the Four Winds this summer to make him forget; he hadn't wanted to come back for another year. And he wasn't forgetting.

They were in the ocean together, yards from shore. The ocean could have been a lake for calmness, so smooth, so gradual, so still. She was wearing a two-piece bathing suit, a peplum, this was a mysteriously fixed detail. They walked on until the water was up to their necks.

All serene. Nothing but two heads on a long shelf of water, a ceramic stillness.

White air. The sun came to them through petals. They looked back over their shoulders to the shoreline. Ethel, sunbathing, traced a lazy figure eight with her hand and turned over on her back. The beach was dotted with legs, breasts, umbrellas, balls, baskets—the usual summer scene. They stood facing each other, Fern and himself, their heads clear of the water, a feathery blue space between their lips. Her hair played about his face like spray

Minnows, tiny sea-pipes, fins and nozzles, nibbled their bellies, backs and legs:

Kiss, kiss.

Kiss.

Mustn't. Their lips mustn't touch. One of the rules. Only the minnows moved between. He was stretched as tight to bursting as the top skin of a drum.

Her suit has billowed away. The water: pellucid, calm. Bless you, child, bless you.

His suit has billowed away. Water stirring faintly now, now churning. We meet as atoms eye to eye, as circling suns enraptured glide . . .

Blue morning. Aunt Ethel had awakened with a dull splitting ache, as if she'd spent the night with her head between sandbags. Morning mouth: awful. Something was eating her, some canker, heartworm—if there were such a thing She lifted the hand mirror from the bed-table. A gout of dust came with it.

With care, she examined her face, then raked her hair with her fingers, noting some rough patches of scalp.

Why not get up with the rest of the house? Find out what the students were up to. Probably goofing off, every one. Most mornings at this time, she turned over and snuggled deeper into the warm. But today her head ached: it was that blasted radio, Tertu's radio had done it.

She raised herself and padded over to the full-length mirror on the closet door. Disrobing, she examined her body coolly, appraising it with the detachment of a by-stander. Her breasts hung, useless, not especially orna-mental. Still, everything seemed in order, she could spot no actual deformity. Nevertheless, she was chilled by what she saw. At that moment her body had taken on the aspect of any other body. Like those clinical photographs of terminal cases and freaks, where the person stood head-on, face and genitals to the camera, an oblong of darkness over the eyes. The nakedness was not in the exposure of genitals but in the blotting-out of eyes, and that the body was perceived without a modicum of love. It all looked like pale and ghostly meat.

She hurried into her underclothes. Counting on the weather to warm up rapidly, Aunt Ethel decided on shorts and chose her striped Italian sweater. Which shoes? Not sneakers today, but something special. Did her knees look middle-aged? Winking with fat? No, her legs were all right, not bad for a woman over forty-five A hundred and nine pounds, she was sticking to it now. She had rather nice legs, if she did say so herself, firm and slim, with none of those blue traceries or filigree patterns that most women her age had. Having babies messed them up. Well, she'd been spared, there was some consolation in it.

Why not break in her new sandals? That would be a lift, she'd wear them for the first time this morning. They weren't her type—so much the better! They were flimsy and frivolous. An aberration: she'd pleased herself by stepping out of character for once. They had T-straps, which lengthened the line of the feet and, since they had heels and the feet sloped downward, added to the slimness of her legs. They had cork soles and funny little cork heels shaped like bobbins.

Time to nudge Chief—well past the breakfast hour. Chief snorted and writhed, mumbled something that sounded like "Boho"—the faker. Then he turned over.

"Nine thirty," she announced, advancing the time by twenty minutes. "Nearly noon. The students must be at work crew. I'm going to have a look." She clapped the door behind her with emphasis.

She started down the steps.

At the half-stage landing she began to skate. She grabbed for the banister rail but miscalculated, collided with nothing, scooped the air. The stairs opened and shut like an accordion. Tilted—rushed up—spun: a jagged-toothed wheel. The pitch was steep and she strained against it to keep from hurtling head over heel. Slap, slap, slap. Her shoes remained fixed to her feet, but one heel gave with a pop—a tiny snap, dwarfed in a cannonade of sound.

She landed on her rump. Shaking, shaking, the stairs still spilling past, her ears seething. The stairs seemed to be chuckling now: *yuk, yuk*—an echo. The little heel was still skipping on its own. The important thing was her spine. Was it injured? No. It might have been. She could have broken her neck. It seemed no accident to her, but the most pointed and personal of insults. She sat for several minutes on the last step, quietly trembling. No one came to ask how she was. No one passed that way. Even so.

The detached heel rested quietly on the floor below. It had torn off unevenly, taking part of the sole. Nothing clean about that break; it couldn't be glued back now or ever.

She made no motion to collect the heel. Let it lie. When her breath was restored to her, she began her slow ascent. She carried her sandals, though she might as well have tossed them straight into the ash bin. Much good they had done her.

Slowly up the steps. Her bare feet made a rude sucking noise against the boards.

At the half-stage landing, where she had first lost her footing, she paused. The floor was still wet and decidedly slippery. She ran the palm of her hand over the boards—they were oily! Strange. Something to look into.

Chief was in the bathroom, behind a barricade of running water. "Don't break your neck when you come down!" she hollered.

"What?" said Chief.

"Go down the back way. There's been an accident on the front stairs."

"What?" said Chief, opening the door a crack.

She explained.

"Okay," he agreed without excitement. He shut the door. Then he opened it once more: an afterthought: "You all right?"

"I will be," she said with conviction.

There was no one else who used those stairs, so she was covered for the moment. She needed something to calm her, a cigarette. She opened one drawer after another, rattling around for one. In mounting desperation, she rummaged through Chief's underwear. There was a box of something— No, only a dress shirt in its cardboard stiffeners. Nothing! Aunt Ethel slammed the last drawer into place. Her own fault this time, she'd hidden the cigarettes from herself. Downstairs in the kitchen maybe? No, no time. No time to lose. Better see to the stairs first, before they dried off.

She went down by the back staircase. Still shaky, she gripped the banister firmly. Her passage was safe and swift.

It wasn't hard to find out whose job the front stairs had been. Housekeeping assignments were posted on the bulletin board near the common room.

Isaiah had been the one. It didn't come as a great surprise.

When she located him in his lab, he was already busy taking blood counts. The other students were still at chores.

"I want you to see something," she announced. Calmly, without any particular expression.

"Could it wait an hour? I'm in the middle of something important."

"I'm afraid not. *This* is important. You'll have to come

now. Before anyone else has a chance to break their necks."

She confronted him with the evidence and waited silently for his reaction.

But there was none. "All right," he said evenly, "I'll get a rag and dry it up." No apology, not a twinge of remorse.

"I'm afraid that won't be enough. You'll have to spare the precious time and start all over again. You used too much oil. It will dull the wood. Wipe it off and start over with less."

"I don't see why I should do it again if it's nearly dry. Once is enough. More than enough, I think."

"What makes you think you have any right to think in this matter? I'm *ordering* you to do it. Understand plain English?"

"I can't. It's the principle of the thing. Like—I mean, this is only a house. Wood and stone. I'll wipe it off and that's the end of it."

"You're telling *me* what the end of it is! I'm going to put such a black mark against your name in my record book you'll never forget it. That's a permanent record."

"All right." He smiled. A sly wisp of a smile hovered over his lips.

She closed her eyes, her face filled with blood. Then her anger knew no bounds. It began with Isaiah and went way beyond him. Had he not been standing there, staring at her, she would have shouted, cried out. Anger moved through her like a parade, a marching band, it came with bugles, bells, pipes, brasses, drums—Christ, the din!

It was perfectly quiet. Staring blankly, saying nothing, Isaiah hitched at the cloth of his crotch.

That did it. She grabbed for his ear, clamped tight, yanking his head from side to side, and—once—battering his temple against the wall, hard enough, just hard enough, to scare them both. "You watch it, boy—you watch it! You've gone too far—" She let him go with no relief, all stifled, nothing spent.

13

THE RAIN CAME DOWN.

"On such a night Captain Hinkley hears the dipping of oars. Then he sees seventeen men, all pale and shining-wet, clamber aboard the Nelson. One—he goes aft to the wheel, one to the stern, one to the watch, two to the halyards—"

"What's the halwats?"

"Shhh . . . some part of the ship. Dummy!"

Tertu dropped a stitch and was busy recouping it. She was slightly deaf and heard the children's interruptions only when she chose.

"The rest cast their lines."

"Were they ghosts, Tertu?"

"That I'm not saying. And that's the end. I told you two stories now. The story of the ghost ship of Gloucester. And the story of the old lady who had one eye and only three tears left to spend, remember? It's double the end, so help me, and well past all bedtimes, too."

Once a week, since the arrival of Doris, Tertu was able to do a bit of baby-sitting for the Homays, freeing them for a night on the town. Doris was the new help from Moosepick, hired to assist in the kitchen.

She was a striking girl. Her eyes were an almost colorless gray, so light they seemed to be depthless and to give back unchanged everything they took in, an unstirred pool. She smiled much of the time. Her smile was wide and slow, arriving too late and lingering too long, so that it stood out at odd moments in the midst of unsmiling matters. She was striking, no denying it, but not really pretty. Her hair was brown with red lights in it, her skin was very white. Although she did her share, she worked with only one hand, for she had only one good arm. Her left arm was withered and shorter than her right and she held it pinched to her side, elbow bent, her dwarf hand tucked in as if the fingers were stitched, the thread drawn tight.

She had some definite notions, notions of beauty. Tertu couldn't make much sense of them. No matter what anybody said, Doris would never wear an apron. But her dresses were no better than aprons, paisleys faded and loose, all swirls and curls, sad mangy blossom prints, the sort of housedresses people put out at fire sales for fifty cents an item or two dollars a rack. She had a way of holding up the fingers of her good hand and becoming lost in admiration for the swank she found there: a silver ring with three pinpoint turquoise stones—some bus depot souvenir. A fair worker in spite of all, Tertu had to admit it. But not much in the way of company, for she spoke even less frequently than Tertu herself, which meant hardly ever. A bit backward, maybe, Tertu wondered from time to time. What did she make of the students? Of Aunt Ethel?

At this point it was common knowledge that Aunt Ethel had some sort of "complaint." Tertu thought it might be one of those "woman's complaints," but she wasn't sure. The trouble seemed to strike Aunt Ethel in the morning and to ease up as the day wore on. Cup of sea water every morning or a glass of rhubarb juice taken regular might be the very thing for it. Steady work and not hankering after things you could never possess, that would cure all the rest. Living within your means, Tertu thought, that's the answer. I do, creatures do, but most folks won't.

Late Tuesday morning of the third week, Aunt Ethel emerged from her room looking terribly sad. Anna and Eddy Bartusek happened to be passing through the corridor at that moment. "Would you come in here?" She beckoned to Anna. "Edward, you too."

It was the first time Anna had ever entered that bedroom. A heavy musty odor clung to the walls: bad sleep and smoke. The curtains were drawn and the shades were flush to the sills. Anna's eyes were full of the light of morning, and it took her a moment to become accustomed to the twilight in the room.

Aunt Ethel leaned, a dense shape, against the bureau. "Would you please take care of it?" She pointed to the birdcage on its gilded stand.

Anna approached the cage for closer inspection, Eddy

close on her heels. Aunt Ethel did not move but continued to indicate with a long arm, stiff as a pointer, where the trouble was. As Anna touched the hood, Aunt Ethel averted her face; for an instant, she swayed. She steadied herself by leaning on the bureau and pretending to fumble for cigarettes.

"Hello?" Anna raised the fringed hood. "Good morning, Larry," she intoned hopefully

There was no response. It occurred to Anna that she hadn't seen the bird in some time and, when last she spoke to him, he hadn't bothered to answer or even to look up. Anna peered closer: nothing doing. The little perch and swing stood empty. The drinking trough was low on water, only a tiny puddle, dull with scurf. She was able to make out a dark mound of some sort, clumped with sawdust, droppings, seeds.

Nothing much to speak of there: a hump—black with a soiled yellow streak, the punctuation of a copper beak, two upended hairpin legs. The feathers were rumpled and clotted. You could have carried off the corpse with a small soup ladle.

"Frank bought him for me. It was our nineteenth anniversary, three years back now. Larry was always with us. Even in the bedroom . . . where everything is personal."

Anna and Eddy exchanged glances, but Anna couldn't make out the message, the light was so bad.

"I can count on you two to clean it out, I'm sure. I have a strong stomach, it's not that. He was like a person to me. Used to stay up with me nights when I couldn't sleep. I'm going to step outside now because—"

Eddy ran down to the broom closet for dustpan and brush. They made short work of it, a few sweeps and it was done. "Am I glad!" Eddy confessed. "That was one sardonic bird. Always wisecracking. Good riddance to him, I say.

"Good morning Larry," Eddy mimicked.

"What you doin'?" Anna piped.

"Stop that!" Eddy again, but the fun quickly trickled away.

Afterwards Anna carried the empty cage out to the front lawn, where Alfred hosed it down.

"Death in the family?" he asked, spraying it from different angles.

Anna nodded. "Not *my* family."

"Didn't know as there was a bird in the house. There you are—clean as a whistle. I'd set it down to dry in the sun for half an hour if I was you."

But Anna hadn't that much time to spare. She held up the cage and swung it like a lantern to and fro. "What kind of flower is that?" Anna pointed.

"Which? Far as I can see you're pointing at weeds."

"This stuff here." Anna lifted a sprig. "See: this yellow and orange. Looks a little like sweet pea. Only sweet pea doesn't grow on a bush."

"That? That there's a wild one. Called spotted touch-me-not."

"Funny name. Wonder why anybody—"

"Right name for it. Petals curl under if you touch 'em. Like some folks, don'tcha know? Real decent from a ways off, but it don't pay to get too close."

A few days after Larry's death, Tertu baked a layer cake, and the students presented Aunt Ethel with an anniversary gift, a new pet. It was Bob Homay's idea. Aunt Ethel and Chief quickly dubbed the kitten "Aorta"—"Ao" for short—because the kitten was fond of leaping up into the air, her back in a high arch. She was cinnamon-colored with a white nose and three white stockings. But, unlike Larry, who stayed put in his cage, Ao couldn't be contained and all of the Four Winds was her domain. They would have to take care to make sure she didn't get beyond the porch and find her way down to the Mouse House.

Before letting the kitten into the house for the first time, Tertu held her fast while Doris gently buttered her paws. The two women seemed to know what they were up to, although everyone else remained mystified. "Got to be done. Done right," was all Tertu would say by way of explanation.

14

RECREATION WAS a problem at the Four Winds. The compulsory baseball game each Saturday evening was generally resented; only a few of the students had any real enthusiasm. They were required to play until the light failed; the evenings were long, and the games seemed interminable.

The teams were called the Basenjis (for a variety of barkless dog), and the Buttercups (for unparalleled aggressiveness). Jerome was a member of the Buttercups, along with such stars as Leo and Isaiah.

Once in a great while, the Buttercups managed to score, by default usually—Eva's loose outfielding or Hans's fumbling as he botanized at third base—but occasionally Eddy's clout or Naomi's speed carried them in for a home run. Eddy was a slugger, erratic but powerful, and Naomi had one saving skill: she was very good at stealing bases. Her only problem was getting to first base.

They played on the town diamond. A few of the locals

with time to kill would sit on the bleachers and razz whichever team was up: "What is this—Ping-Pong? Badminton? Let's play *ball!*"

That was bad enough, but worse was in store. At the beginning of the third week, the students were encouraged to spend half an hour a day swimming. When no one responded to encouragement, they were ordered to do so. Baseball, however dreary, turned out to be far more agreeable than swimming, for the ocean was frigid.

"Melting slush," said Isaiah. It was only a slight exaggeration.

"Got to keep you all in condition," Aunt Ethel insisted. "Fifteen minutes—at the very least."

Jerome studied the others as they went in. Herb Smith made a direct plunge. "Pretty hairy!" he warned, thrashing about. Naomi started out with a slow amble, then began to trot and, finally, splashing herself all over, ducked to the ears. She swam furiously, back and forth, between the shoals and the bluffs.

Chief posed at the edge of the sea, hands on waist. "I do this once a year," he announced, "for my wife." He extended one shapely leg, then another, then went forward. Halfway in, he reversed himself and rushed upon Aunt Ethel. She fended him off with both hands. "*Get—*" she cried, "get on with you!" Husband and wife stared at each other and flashed their teeth. Chief returned to the water. "Practice what you preach!" he tossed over his shoulder.

Aunt Ethel followed him, keeping her distance. She lowered herself in fixed increments, as though descending a staircase. By the time she was submerged to the waist,

Chief was already nearing the shoals. He was an energetic swimmer and made waves as he went. On the sunny ledge of the Cormorant, Eva lay warming herself. Chief rose from the foam and stood above her, streaming. She shrieked with surprise.

Swimming parallel to the bluffs, Aunt Ethel staked out a middle lane for herself. By now nearly everyone was in. Chief and Eva were racing in the open water beyond the shoals.

After a very few minutes, Aunt Ethel withdrew. She toweled briskly and turned to the laggers: "Well now, I'm waiting."

Jerome was still dallying with the knots in his shoelaces, and Isaiah stood in his socks, looking out.

"Well?"

Isaiah's attack was piecemeal, even dainty. He took many, many mincing steps, getting accustomed by degrees, pausing for ankles, pausing for calves, pausing for knees, splashing the small of his back, postponing the inevitable final step, which only served to portion out the pain.

Submerged to the shoulders, he did not swim; clearly he didn't know how. Aunt Ethel watched intently as he faked a swim by trotting rapidly to and fro in the shallows, stooped over so it wouldn't show how shallow, and making vigorous stroking motions with his arms. She was so absorbed in the spectacle that she seemed to have forgotten all about Jerome.

Between Aunt Ethel and Isaiah, a certain tension was apparent, undefined but persistent. By this time the incident on the stairs was well known. When Aunt Ethel passed Isaiah in the hallway, people glanced from one to the other, expecting something. They were not often disappointed. It was like a duet: she scolded, he hummed a tune; she insisted, he answered with a *presto*, a *saraband* —no answer at all—so it went on and on. She could not force him to pay attention. She had only the power of reprisal, no controlling power. She sensed her own weakness and rejoiced in any weakness she could discover in him.

"I'm still waiting, Jerome—" Without warning, Aunt Ethel wheeled around.

There was, then, to be no escape. Jerome decided that Herb's way was best and dove in. He'd watched all the others go before him and thought he knew what to expect. Yet nothing had prepared him for the impact of that water: it was direct knowledge. He was stung.

15

AFTER SWIMMING, the students were required to spend a full hour in the sun. It wasn't hard to figure out why. Parents were due up the next weekend, and the Elosons wanted their charges looking bronze and sleek.

The sunbath proved to be a welcome change. Even a few days made a perceptible difference. And even Hans, the palest of the lot, had lost what Aunt Ethel called "that sickly bluish-greenish pallor" and was on his way to looking human. After a week, the cheeks of the students were glowing.

"I can *feel* it—hey, Leo, I can feel the continental drift!" Alex cried, placing his palms flat on the grass.

Leo Proudhon gave one of his affected laughs, all *tsisps* and *tseeps:* a scissors. He laughed with his front palate, tonguetip and nose. The students had secretly named him "Himander" for "him-and-her."

Naomi stretched out on her back, basking in the warmth, breathing in the musk of a summer afternoon and thinking of nothing much. How flat she was even now! She could still lie comfortably on her stomach if she wanted to; none of the other girls could.

Would she never look her age? Her round face, smooth and untroubled, punctuated only by cheerful dimples, read "no experience" for all the world to see. She wanted a serious face so that people would take her seriously. She longed for intricacies, crimps, furrows, hollows in the cheeks and grave shadows under the eyes, congruence— some outward show of the deep inner complexity she was sure she possessed. Instead, she had the face of a ten- or eleven-year-old child. Naomi had once heard of a girl of fifteen whose bone age was eight. At times, she felt within herself an even more discordant mixture of ages, as if her bone age, mental age, and emotional age were widely spaced and belonged to separate people.

"Hey, Jerome, it's your move." Jerome and Hans Tivonen were playing Go. Jerome had been watching Naomi, studying her.

He was a very private person, staring much and saying little. He confided only to his diary. The diary was his little secret, or so he imagined. Everyone knew about it but no one let on. The only real secret was where the book was hidden away; Johnny hadn't been able to stay awake long enough to find out.

Must be a very boring book, Naomi thought, full of pious sentiment and Go strategy. And what else? Wonder if I'm in it. . . .

She peered up at the linden trees and the great pines whitened with beard. Lying out on the grass after her swim, her blood booming, Naomi required nothing, and the passion to work escaped her. She closed her eyes and studied the pattern of capillaries on her inner eyelids until their incandescence pained her and she was forced to blot out the light with her hand. Afterwards she opened her eyes and sat up. She stared blindly at first. The sun seemed to have smeared everything; she blinked and blinked.

It wasn't only the sun; there was a blur of activity on all sides. Eddy, Herb and Jenise held a Frisbee war on the far lawn. Vito lounged on the sidelines, his ear plugged in to a transistor radio. Alex Nesselroth roused himself and agreed on some rounds of blitz chess with Joel. They were ruthless and noisy about it. Hans sat in the shade of a large ash and played an endless game of Go with Jerome. They played on graph paper, drawing shaded and empty circles at the intersections of the squares for their black and white stones. Whenever any of the stones were captured, they erased the circles. The players were a study in black and white, for Hans was excessively fair and had to remain in the shade, while Jerome, who was tanning quickly, sat opposite him in the full blaze of the sun. They sat with their legs crossed, facing each other in silence.

They were slow: in contrast to the chess players, theirs seemed to be a game of great civility, small increments and infinite patience. The chess players kept sneaking glances in their direction, obviously fascinated and, at the same time, put out by what they must have felt to be a display of one-upmanship. After a while they left off their own boisterous warfare and clustered round the silent Go players, who never looked up from their grid. The game was truly endless and the players would pick it up, day after day, just where they'd left off. The graph paper came in handy for, where stones would have jostled, their penciled positions remained fixed from one day to the next.

Tom Li played the harmonica, simple tunes and not very well. Johnny Mendez came out in one of those dark velvet fedoras, very broad-brim, that Naomi was used to seeing on the subway that went through Harlem. It had a violet sash of gathered silk and gave him a look of instant menace. Johnny spent his time walking from group to group, settling on his haunches and chatting. But as soon as he saw Isaiah bearing down upon them, he was up and on his way. "Uh oh," he warned, "here comes guess who—on all eight pairs of stalking legs. Note the determination of the fused head and thorax—great concentration there. Observe the delicate chelicerae and pedipalps. Yipes!" And off Johnny scooted.

Isaiah never settled. Pacing back and forth, he made observations on everything. He had a habit of pulling up fistfuls of grass and breaking off leaves as he spoke, his hands in perpetual motion. Naomi was certain he did not know what his fingers were doing. His shredding was an accompaniment to his conversation, which was mostly criticism and complaint. The sunbathing was a waste of time, he said. If he were allowed to play his fiddle now, it would be different. But he wasn't allowed. Why was Tom allowed to play his harmonica? Because he *wasn't* serious? What kind of sense did that make?

"Know what I think? I think she's got a weak spot for music. That's why I get on her nerves—it's my fiddle she can't stand. No reason for it unless she was a real sucker for it once. You know, great hate after great love."

"That's crazy," Naomi said flatly.

Isaiah shrugged, didn't insist. "It's possible," he said, "it's just possible. Stranger things have happened."

"You know what I don't understand, Isaiah—I can't figure out why, if you're so crazy about music—"

"Why I'm here mucking up my hands with dissection?" He shrugged. "It's really mixed up. A lot of it's money, but not all. It looks good for getting into med school, right? Nothing wrong with being a doctor—a good career where you feel useful, people always telling you how useful you ought to feel. Who doesn't want to feel useful and make a lot of money? Be crazy not to. You think I'm crazy? You're not even listening. You asked a question and you're not even listening to the answer."

"That's not true—I was listening."

It was partly true. Ask a simple question and he buzzes like a hornet, she thought. She had been listening, but began to back off as soon as she realized she'd triggered an angry nerve.

"You asked me what I'm doing here. The long and short of it is—I'd like to fiddle, but even good musicians starve. And I don't know how good I really am. That's why my family—"

"Oh, families . . . I know how they are," Naomi agreed with a big sigh, "they *make* problems." It was one of her favorite subjects and, without waiting for permission from Isaiah, she plunged into her own trials.

Then, somehow, without her knowing how it happened, the conversation came full circle. Did she know that a fiddle was made of more than eighty separate pieces and four different kinds of wood? She didn't. It was a fact—

rosewood, ebony, maple and pine. Really? A fact. "Maybe that's why it sounds so plangent here in the woods. Wood to wood. Sympathetic resonance—whadaya think?"

"I think I've never heard the word 'plangent' before. Maybe I've read it—I guess I know what it means. But nobody, but nobody, ever *says* it, Isaiah."

"So what? I do," he answered.

Did she realize all the trouble people took to find the right kind of wood for a violin, not too hard, not too soft, to give out sounds that were pure, brilliant and sonorous? They usually cut from the south side of the tree in December or January, when the sap was believed to stand still. Wasn't that a peculiar notion? The wood had to be seasoned for at least six or seven years. Naomi hadn't known, she couldn't appreciate, she didn't realize and, by and by, she ceased listening altogether. Not by intention, not by any act of will, but all imperceptibly, unconsciously, and by degrees. What Isaiah was saying had nothing to do with her; it was nothing but static as far as she was concerned, and she tuned him out.

Naomi was the worst possible listener. She watched Isaiah's mouth moving and guessed the broad context, but the words weren't coming through. And then she lost track of the context. There were so many competing sounds: a bird or insect whirring like a tiny buzz saw; a lobster boat churning, circling round a trap; gulls, shrill cries. Suddenly, by a transition she'd missed, he was naming names familiar to her. It sounded like a subway litany, a hymn to Brooklyn. "Far Rockaway! Canarsie! Bensonhurst! Flatbush Avenue!" Naomi began to giggle and looked up, hoping her laughter was catching. But Isaiah responded with a cold, curious deadpan. She'd missed something. What? Had he been talking about the movements of a contemporary symphony or about subway stops? Impossible to tell now.

"Except when he's fiddling he moves around like a loose assemblage of parts," Naomi had written in her last letter home. "I wouldn't be surprised if he combed his hair with his pencil or his fork. He's from Flatbush and Jewish, a nice Jewish boy. Believe me, he isn't that nice. I'm not going to tell you his last name. It's my only way of making sure you won't go snooping, asking around for family connections. (We aren't all related, you know.)"

He was so utterly pathetic, a walking cartoon prodigy complete with heavy glasses, acne, library pallor and a habit of speech as nervous and compulsive, as untranslatable, as a successsion of tics. If only he could see himself! While everyone else went around barefoot, Isaiah kept on his dark socks, which was the final touch as far as Naomi was concerned.

On Wednesday afternoon of that week, the students formed a line outside the Eloson's private dining room and awaited approval for equipment needed in their solo projects. This was the last step before finally getting under way. It had taken enough time. Since they had gone over their lists with their sponsors beforehand, they expected Chief to do nothing but add a formal stamp of approval. Naomi had reduced her tissue-culture list to the barest minimum before presenting it to Lebret; none of it was negotiable:

1. Dry sterilization apparatus
2. Autoclave for steam sterilization
3. Muffle furnace
4. Filtration apparatus (vacuum)
5. Stills (2)
6. Plastic dust shield
7. Hot plate
8. Special glassware: watch glasses, etc.

Naomi stood in the middle of the line. As the students ahead of her went through, she learned that the interviews all had the same pattern. Each student underwent a brief interrogation, each interrogation began with a little preface. First of all, Aunt Ethel's presence called for a word or two. She was sitting at Chief's side as his constant helpmeet—did the student have any objection?

Under the circumstances, what objection could there be?

Naomi emerged miraculously intact, but Isaiah's requests for his anoxia project were radically trimmed. He wanted a decompression chamber for greater flexibility and control; Kamin had agreed that it was a sound idea. The Elosons didn't see why he wouldn't be satisfied by a simple vacuum bell jar with a small pump and manometer attachments. "All I want to produce is oxygen deprivation, not complete and utter deprivation," Isaiah argued, his voice shrill. "It's an absolutely *critical* period of embryonic development!" The words "deprivation" and "critical" carried down the length of the hallway.

The Elosons were not impressed. It was no use repeating the same thing over and over: would he please lower his voice? Isaiah offered to ask Kamin whether he could work over at Spemann Lab, where a decompression chamber was available. Aunt Ethel thought this would set a very bad precedent. In the end, Isaiah had to settle for the vacuum jar. "Small beginnings," said Chief, "that's the way we all started."

Afterwards speculation began. Rumor had it that, although the Elosons had directed the summer program since its inception, they had not been the Alkahest's first choice. But the fact that they were childless had worked in their favor. It was assumed that they would be able to give their undivided attention to the students. A sense of being second or third choice would explain Aunt Ethel's anxiety to prove herself by keeping costs down. Help explain, but not justify—there was a difference.

On Thursday the first surgery schedules were posted. Each of the students was to be involved at some point in the summer. The usual progression was: observer, third assistant, second assistant, anesthetist, first assistant. Naomi was to begin on Sunday of the fifth week.

With the distribution of equipment, their lab assignments were finalized.

Joel kept on pestering Naomi day after day, yanking off her hair bows and running away with them. Naomi made a point of tying up her hair in shoelaces, since she had a horror of ribbons but sufficient vanity to avoid plain rubber bands. She'd brought up a batch of shoelaces in every color, including plaid. Her mother never stopped telling her what an affectation this was, but call it what they would, Naomi felt that shoelaces suited the kind of person she was—no frills, yet not without color. And now someone else was fond of shoelaces.

Their skirmishes were public; the other students couldn't help noticing. "I'd call that love, wouldn't you?" Evie teased. There was a chorus of bright remarks on the subject.

"And I'd call it softening of the brain," said Naomi, loud enough for Joel to get an earful. But Joel was off, halfway down the hall, whistling to himself.

16

THAT WEEKEND, families were free to visit the Four Winds. Naomi's parents combined the journey with three days' vacation on Cape Cod and arrived in a festive mood. It was not to last long.

"The Elosons seem like very nice people. Easygoing sort," her father observed.

"Do they?" said Naomi.

When she tried to explain how the students passed their time, her father nodded thoughtfully. "I don't know, I guess it's a good idea. They must know what they're doing." He said this more than once. "I guess you're making some friends. Kids with the same interests, right?"

Naomi's mother never made a secret of how unhappy she was. "What a *timtum!*" she said the moment she met Isaiah. "That must be the boy you wrote about."

"And get a look at you," she turned to Naomi, "do you see yourself? When did *you* comb your hair last? And with what, may I ask? Your fingers? Surely not a comb? What a mess! What gets me mad is—it's such a *calcu-*

lated mess. Do you go out of your way to muss up your hair like that?"

Why didn't she cut her hair? When was she going to stop biting her nails? A perfectly infantile habit like thumb-sucking—did she realize that? Mothering, smothering, it went on and on.

No surprise then when she received a letter, complete with envelope and address, on Saturday afternoon. At home, whenever this happened, the letter would be slipped under the door and Naomi would exacerbate the situation by slipping the answer back in the same fashion.

It was the usual purple prose. Her mother pressed it into her hand as she was going upstairs to change for dinner. Of course, she could have said it all to Naomi's face rather than writing a letter as if they were miles apart, but she knew that they would both start a scene, and preferred the distance and neutrality of paper, a buffer zone:

Dear Naomi,

Please let's pretend. Put on some nice clean clothes, change your sneakers, comb your hair and pin it down with some bobby pins and act sociable.

It's such a short visit, surely you can humor me for a little while. Maybe then when I've gone back home I can convince myself that you have some feeling, if only for childhood memories. I haven't even one whole day left with you. Give a crumb.

Your loving,
Mom

The usual melodramatics. Naomi tried her best to oblige, simply to close off further discussion, not because she agreed with the principles involved. She changed her sneakers to loafers and gave her hair a swat. But no bobby pins, that was asking too much.

On Sunday they went into town. They stopped for ice cream at Bill Cutliffe's soda shop, then visited all the tourist traps. Her mother bought a miniature cedar chest with a velvet pincushion inside, and a sachet full of balsam. Her father bought a can opener with an abalone handle and a sweat shirt with a map on it for David, his favorite nephew. He toyed with the notion of sending a can of country air back to some friends in Manhattan. It had marks for perforations at the top so that the air wouldn't escape all at once. The label read:

—8 OZ. PURE NATIVE AIR—
DELIGHTFUL AROMA
Cinnamon roses, cowpat, seaweed and fern,
Swamp grass and pine,
Sassafras and old fish bait, salt
of the sea.

Not only did they purchase the can of native air, they sent it on the spot, since there was a postcard attached. A toy birchbark canoe for another of Naomi's cousins, and then they called it a day.

After her parents left, Naomi began to feel a little lost, in spite of herself. A momentary dislocation, she told herself: it'll pass. She reviewed the week and decided that it hadn't been a bad one, all in all. It occurred to her, looking back, that Aunt Ethel had been unusually quiet the past few days. Had she been ill? Naomi knew that Aunt Ethel was taking a lot of medicine because she'd been called into her bedroom on Tuesday. The bureau was full of little bottles—blue pills, yellow pills, capsules with orange stripes. Sometimes her speech was slurry.

"You're the youngest we've ever taken," Aunt Ethel had confided, as though it were news. "Show us what you can do!"

But she made precious few appearances all that week and, when she did, wore sunglasses, forgetting to take them off even inside the house. They were celebrity glasses, big as saucers. "She's hiding behind them. That's why movie stars wear them," Isaiah speculated. "Rainy eyes."

In all those days there'd been only one run-in worthy of notice. Isaiah was involved. The two of them seemed out to *get* one another. But, this time, few of the students found any right on Aunt Ethel's side.

It happened because Isaiah used to practice his violin during the evening social hour. He used the empty seminar room. Aunt Ethel told him he'd have to practice somewhere else, but didn't tell him where. Isaiah tried a number of places, settling finally on the half-stage landing on the staircase. He couldn't have found a worse location. The sound carried even better than before. They could hear Isaiah all over the house and, much as some of them liked Mendelssohn, they weren't sure Aunt Ethel did.

"He sure plays awfully Jewish," said Joel.

"And what does that mean?" Naomi demanded.

"Oh, you know, *schmaltz*."

Naomi guessed she did know.

As soon as the last parent left, the week-long truce was broken. The students were sitting down for supper when Bob Homay rose to make an announcement. He asked to see Eddy Bartusek and Alex Nesselroth, the captains of the two baseball teams, as soon as they were done eating. He warned all the rest that they had better start playing a more serious game next Saturday evening. In the middle of his speech, Aunt Ethel entered. She stood up at the front of the room, her back to the big bay window.

After Bob Homay had finished, she continued surveying the group in silence. One or two of the students began to eat and she stared at them until they left off and raised their eyes.

The students puzzled at her sudden appearance. Normally they didn't see Aunt Ethel at all during meals, which she took in the private dining room with Chief. The Homays ate with the students, but once a week the Elosons and the Homays lunched together in the small dining room and discussed administrative matters. It was clear that Aunt Ethel's visit signified something important.

The subject was housekeeping, and the matter was urgent. She wanted the students to pay attention, point by point, because this was one place where housework was not made light of or demeaned. She extracted a small sheet of notepaper from the pocket of her slacks and, pointing with her forefinger, began ticking off items in a long bill of particulars.

Naomi sneaked a quick dip of gravy while it was still hot.

Item one: Dishes were to be done in shorter time. Dish crew always meant five—two washing, two drying, one clearing tables and mopping the floor. She'd found only one person drying dishes the night before—why was that?

Aunt Ethel made her point without mentioning names, and the question might have passed as rhetorical had not Isaiah blurted out that he knew very well that he was scheduled for "the drying brigade." Unfortunately, he had seven P.M. blood counts to do on his project for Dr. Kamin and there couldn't be any tampering with *that* time schedule. Alex Nesselroth had agreed to a trade-off arrangement, Isaiah doubling for Alex during the lunch hour.

"There are no trade-offs, no special arrangements!" Aunt Ethel countered at once. "As for Dr. Kamin, I'll fix him. I'm not going to let a man standing on two canes tell me how to run my house! You'll have to learn to make time, Isaiah, same as everybody else. That goes for everyone here."

Isaiah opened his mouth, closed it, let out nothing but a little packet of air in reply.

Second point: The kitchen floor was left dirty day after day. There were finger smudges on the cupboard door. If anyone needed lessons on wet-mopping, Aunt Ethel would be only too happy to oblige. She had no choice but to give black marks to every member of the dish crew for this. She didn't know or care whose fault it was.

Then on to the real lecture: If the students couldn't keep the kitchen clean, how on God's earth could they keep their labs clean? If they couldn't keep their labs clean, how could they know whether their results were correct? If they couldn't tell whether their results were correct, then what kind of scientists were they? If they were the future of American science, then what kind of a future could American science have?

The students sat there, peering down wistfully at their plates, at suppers growing cold.

There was a brief postscript addressed to the Homays on the subject of punctuality. It could have been gone into privately, but Aunt Ethel must have had reasons for taking it up in front of everyone else. The Homays sat through this public chastisement very humbly, like poor relations at a feast. They had come in late after driving those students who had no visitors into town. They'd taken nearly half the group and used two cars.

Later on in the evening, when matters seemed to have simmered down, Tom Li knocked on the door of Naomi's lab.

"Hey—you seen Isaiah?"

"Not lately. What gives?"

"The Grand Moghul wants him, that's all I know. She wants him pretty bad. By the way you're not supposed to be up here. It's the social hour, remember?"

"Well, you haven't seen me and I haven't seen him."

A few days after that, Aunt Ethel forbade Isaiah to practice anywhere in the house. "I'm putting my foot down," she announced, "it's for your own good." She told him that scientists ought to concentrate on one thing at a time. And, besides, nine to ten was the social hour. Why wasn't he socializing?

Isaiah snapped shut his case without bothering to answer and stomped out of the house.

A long silence followed. Then, after an interval, the sounds of tuning-up coming from somewhere out on the lawn, and a shivery, silvery trilling. Mozart, was it? All points and curls, full of humor, almost mocking.

Also in retaliation: a jig, a polka, Vivaldi—fast and fiery. Anything, Naomi guessed, to keep warm.

Naomi stood on the porch, listening. Some blocks of light from the window fell upon the lawn, making a frame, an enclosure of bright, pitched squares and sharp criss-crossing lines. Isaiah was not within the pattern. He must have been playing from memory, out beyond the lights, in darkness.

Aunt Ethel listened from the doorway. Her head ached: he mocked her. She had never felt so scorned. Never—or only once before. Frank, for a joke, had made a tape recording of one of her angry tirades and played it back to her after her anger was cool—her own voice mocking her.

17

"A HOUSE OF disjoint passions," Jerome had written in one of his lab notebooks, preserving the phrase for its sound if not its sense. He was dimly convinced of its truth long before he could say why.

"A house of secret eating," he added later in a small, collapsed hand. He recognized that writing; it looked like the scribbling he did, often with eyes closed, long after he had finished with his journal, waking suddenly in the dead of night and falling back to sleep at once. Telegrams, jokes, congested music—all he could snatch from dreams that eluded him and seemed important. Sometimes the messages were heavily encoded and he was unable to crack them afterwards. "Someone crying 'help!' or a cat in heat. Hard to tell which." Or: "A Silurian sea bottom where giant molluscs browse and I—" (the rest illegible). At times they were so detached he hadn't a clue to go on: "chill silicon breasts," or the single word "costive."

Then there were the times when he felt that something

momentous had been disclosed and he'd wake to find that he hadn't been able to keep his lines spaced, and all the words had come out in a single line or tangle, superimposed, forever indecipherable.

But "secret eating"? The phrase had definite resonances. When he stopped trying to remember, the incident came back to him.

At the beginning of the summer, Aunt Ethel had taken custody of all student medications. This was a reasonable gesture: she was responsible for the students' welfare. As a former nurse, she had regularly dispensed drugs. Most of the students involved were happy enough to have their medication doled out at the prescribed intervals; it was one less thing to remember.

Jerome's case was a little different. His medication, an antihistamine with sedative properties, was not to be taken regularly, but only when needed. Even so, Aunt Ethel thought it best not to make an exception for him. Not that she didn't trust Jerome; she assured him that she did. But she thought it best to put temptation out of harm's way as far as the other students were concerned— why put ideas in their heads? Aunt Ethel showed Jerome where the bottle would be kept: in the kitchen cupboard, next to the bread box.

During the first week he had resorted to it once. Then for a long span he'd been free of symptoms. Until late one Sunday night, when he'd woken with a headache. Sudden drop in temperature, he decided, reaching for the second blanket. But the headache persisted and was followed by a long spasm of sneezing.

"For Chrissake!" Johnny rapped out.

Jerome bundled into a sweater and socks, and crept downstairs.

The door to the small dining room was open. The room was in darkness, only a blue spill from the television screen seeping over a chair, an expanse of cluttered table, and Aunt Ethel's lap. She was wrapped in a blanket; her hands were hidden under it. She sat without moving, as if under some enchantment; her face was bathed in an underwater light; her back was in darkness, turned to the door.

Reception was none too clear. Someone seemed to be baking a string of pearls in a blueberry pie, that was all Jerome could make out. He went on past, heading for the kitchen.

He withdrew two capsules while he was at it, then a third for good measure. Enough of this midnight foraging. He went back the way he'd come.

Some sort of kissing marathon was on as he passed by the television on his return trip. The contestants clung and fastened. Their lips must have been rubbery and tasteless.

Hearing something, Aunt Ethel swung round. An arm shot out for the light, then, an inch from the lamp, withdrew. She moved forward, stumbling over the blanket in her haste to blot something out— Too late. The evidence was all about, the remains of her midnight snack scattered over the long table: some slices of bread with crusts unbroken (she'd only eaten out the centers); a litter of cherry pits and stems; a watermelon rind in a soup bowl,

gnawed to the outer skin; a half-empty box of bonbons—
the delicate frilled cups were strewn everywhere, like
petals.

He couldn't remember what she said next.

Afterwards, Jerome was uncertain whether he'd been
dreaming or waking. Nothing in Aunt Ethel's manner
hinted that he'd detected her in a compromising position.
Perhaps she'd forgotten. Jerome had wakened the next
morning with the thick head and slow limbs of one who
has been well and truly drugged. But he woke with the
first bell, so his sleep couldn't have been that heavy. He
never found the other two capsules, although he was certain he wouldn't have swallowed all three at once.

Their late-night encounter had the airtight logic of a
dream: that passionless eating was one with the numb
kissing, the murky blue light from the television screen
might have been light from some abyssal zone of the sea
or of the mind. Jerome's waking life rarely had so much
cohesion and often seemed less real, as paper-thin and
abridged as a road map compared with a journey.

He could not resolve the incident. Nor was he able to
forget it or charm it away. "A devouring woman," he
wrote.

"With a stone loaf," he added. He wasn't sure how he
had arrived at this, but he was sure that it was so.

18

ANNA HOMAY WAS SLOW in coming to the inescapable conclusion: there were no weekends at the Four Winds. The students worked as they did on other days; they rushed this way and that, crisp and official in their white jackets, clipboards tucked under their arms, carrying on with their usual strange activities. Every Saturday night there was a baseball game on the town field, ending up with ice cream at a drive-in stand. And that was it, the sum total of possible diversions. Those who wanted to go to church on Sunday had to make up time and arrange for their own transportation. At the beginning there was a small group, but as the summer progressed only Jerome went. Anna usually drove him into town. He was a quiet boy, a thoroughly restful young person. Secretive, of course, terribly secretive, you never really knew what he was thinking. He *was* thinking, that you could tell; if his furious blinking was any index, there was nothing really quiet within. He had a slight stammer when he started to speak but lost it as he gained momentum. A nice boy.

One day differed from another not a jot. Every morning, Saturdays and Sundays included, they woke to martial music, the voice of their drill sergeant, Aunt Ethel, commanding sweep-up in the hall. All the students had grumbled about the housework at first but, quickly realizing that complaint was to no avail, did their best to have done with it as speedily as possible. Only Isaiah did not learn but continued to complain at the top of his voice. Once Anna passed Isaiah's work crew in the hallway, three students on their hands and knees, scrubbing baseboards. Isaiah was declaiming, calling heaven to witness: "Who are we doing penance for, anyway? And why? I'd like to know."

What a place! The amount of time spent in housecleaning operations really was disproportionate. Anna was perfectly familiar with the Puritan maxim that cleanliness was close to godliness, but what that had to do with their case at the Four Winds, bastion of science and secularism, she couldn't begin to fathom. What Anna wished for Aunt Ethel was a house as cold, perfect and empty as a home-furnishings exhibit. Stainless-steel floors. Machine-washable polyurethane chairs and everything else. Dirt colors so as not to show the dirt. Would that cure this frenzy to scrub, scour, unspot? Anna doubted it.

Monday—Monday again, Anna reviewed the days. It wasn't like being at home. It was more like house arrest. But she'd managed to spend an evening on the town, just Bob and herself, twice now, thanks to the arrival of Doris. If Anna was able to make it out and back again between nine thirty and eleven thirty in the morning, she was perfectly free to go out. She had to be back in time to help set up for lunch. Afternoons were hopeless. By the time Jim and Susie had settled down for naps, preparations for supper were well underway.

Bob was no help at all; it was a waste of breath trying to talk to him. "You'll have to work things out for yourself," he said, "like I do." She knew he had his own harassments, but at least he had space to act if he so chose. Anna, for her part, just stewed in her coop. If the children were hungry in the hours between official mealtimes, and they almost always were, Anna couldn't very well sneak down to the kitchen to forage. So she kept a stash of animal crackers and lollies, and they had their own retinue of ants. Luckily Aunt Ethel didn't inspect the Homay quarters.

When they got thirsty there was always water from the tap. No juices or milk, since Anna had no way of keeping ice in the room, and she wasn't allowed in the kitchen until preparations for serving a meal were under way and her help was required. All Anna could do was to slap and yell once animal crackers and lollies had lost their effect.

Nap time. Anna stretched out on her bed and lay there like something killed. Her blouse clung to her skin. She couldn't go up to the roof and try for a tan because Jim or Susie might wake and start squalling. The Four Winds was an unfriendly house for children. Anna got so little sun that she was the same sallow, yellow person she'd been all winter. When she got back home, she could hear her friends saying: "Where you been, you poor thing? Shut up indoors all that time? Weren't you able to manage any vacation at all?" And she'd reply: "Listen, I might not have gotten any sun, but what an adventure I had!"

What an adventure! She lay back, moist, fertile, faceless. Here I am, she announced to the ceiling, a busy woman, busy domesticating chaos. No, an idle woman, a luxurious woman. My body all my wealth, an odalisque. She assumed a reclining position, recumbent on one hip, head like a blown fruit. Not very convincing.

Aunt Ethel, she imagined, was napping in earnest. The poor woman didn't sleep much at night, not lately. The television was buzzing all night long. Aunt Ethel did most of her sleeping or resting in between meals in the daytime. That was one of the reasons the Homay children had to tiptoe through the house during legitimate waking hours.

It reminded Anna of the time, years back, when her grandmother suffered her first stroke. The old woman used television as her night-light and kept it going down the hours, a pale shadow-show, a third carbon of life, but the best she could manage, the closest she could come. She would wake and sleep fitfully; sleep would snatch her unawares, but only for moments at a time. She would wake and find people still moving, laughing, talking, weeping. And so she would wake assured, knowing that life moved about her continuously and that nothing would die in her room, not that night. The old woman lingered for years and, with each year, the greater her fear of the dark became. It was a foretaste, a presentiment of the form her death would surely take, darkness and paralysis. Paralysis, which meant being a prey to whatever moved.

All this was understandable in Anna's grandmother, a

woman in her seventies at the time of her first stroke. But it didn't begin to explain why Aunt Ethel, a woman still so clearly in her prime, with so much waking life to live, chose to live it at one remove. Anna pondered it but found herself no wiser for the effort.

Nothing seemed to give the woman joy. Maybe Larry had, but Anna wasn't even sure of that. The kitten wasn't solving anything. Mostly, she ignored it. Anna heard her speaking to Ao directly only once. "You scratch, you nip —that's your affection." Ao was scrabbling at the floorboards, chasing her own tail up and down the hall, intent on nothing else. "You don't talk—you don't give milk or eggs—what good *are* you?"

She suffered terribly from headaches, she explained to Anna. "Half-headaches," she called them. Migraine. It figured. No children. That figured, too. It all figured. Only her husband and her husband's vocation for company, any drug store dreambook could work it out easily.

Once Anna had surprised her performing the most exotic ritual, something so intimate Anna's glance had sheared away. But Aunt Ethel had forced her to notice: "See! I want you to see—I do it every morning. I'm proud of doing what I do for Frank. Do you love your husband as I love mine? Do you, Anna?" She was stuffing his socks into her blouse, between her breasts, to warm them.

"Well? Do you?"

Anna found herself at a loss for words. Fortunately, Aunt Ethel went right on talking, some strange mood upon her.

"I made him what he is today."

And what is he? Anna wondered to herself.

As if she'd heard, Aunt Ethel began to rattle forth his résumé: "M.D., Sc.D., F.A.C.S.—I put him through medical school by working night shifts. I ironed his shirts for him. I bought his shirts for him so there'd be something to iron. He'd been living in chinos and jerseys. Hadn't a penny to his name. Now he's a rich man, a full professor of surgery, medical consultant to the Air Force, one of the world's top ten experts in heart bypasses and prosthetic heart valves. He's a generalist, one of the very few left. An author, too, and he's written books outside his field—*What's New in Transplants, Living with Colostomy* and *Bioengineering Aspects of the Healing Wound.* The bioengineering one he did with a team of experts from three fields. Those books aren't bestsellers, but they're going to change your life, my life, certainly the lives of these kids here. A big man, I made him big."

"You should take a lot of credit for that," said Anna.

But Aunt Ethel didn't seem to hear, lost in her own thoughts, thinking aloud. "He's the one who didn't want children, you know," she said more to the air than to Anna. "He wanted to give everything to his career."

"Ah," said Anna.

"Not only his career—he wanted to be free. I know he plays around," said Aunt Ethel to her shoes, "don't you think I know?" She looked up, querying, then down again. "It doesn't mean a thing. It's only wanting back all those lost years, all the good years lost in making his way. For all I know, he might have made a pass at you." Now she was asking outright. But not waiting for an answer, not risking it. "If he does, I've only one thing to ask, Anna. Don't tell me about it—it wouldn't be news. So

that's agreed, then. And, another thing, I'd appreciate it if
you kept what I'm telling you between ourselves, just
between us girls. I think I've said more than I should. Can
I count on you?"

Anna nodded. She was aware that Chief was an unusually handsome man, a man used to being noticed. She'd
been aware of it from the first. But he presented no real
danger to her. He had the kind of good looks Anna would
rather gaze on from a distance; he awakened no interest in
closer personal contact. It was one of Anna's quirks. Per-
fection left her admiring, cold, unstirred; what endeared a
man to her were the flaws, the secret soft places. Anyhow,
she couldn't recall any passes, not even the most tentative
hand on the knee. Not even the preliminaries. But then—
she did recall something. Once, when they were sitting by
themselves. It was after one of their weekly "administrative lunches" in the Elosons' private dining room. Aunt
Ethel and Bob had gone off to discuss some matter of
mops and pails. Anna and Chief sat on across from each
other, the remains of their lunch between them. They sat
on, heavy with heat and digestion.

Chief stared, following her least gesture with his eyes.
Anna kept her sights demurely fixed on his cable-knit
chest.

Then he said: "You ought to smile sometimes, Anna.
You've got such a sunny face."

He smiled.

She produced a smile.

They continued, idiotically, staring and grinning until
Anna's smile began to ache; it didn't feel the least bit
happy. Chief's mouth went slack but he continued star-

ing. Now he looked melancholy. Her heart went out to him.

Slowly, his eyes moved over Anna's face, over her bare arms, and she could feel them move, as though his eyelashes were grazing her skin. Then he lowered his eyeglasses and placed them, decisively, face down in his mashed potatoes. The gesture was invested with such cadence, mischief and mystery, and he looked up so yearningly out of such dancing eyes, that Anna was convinced it meant nothing less than an invitation to a striptease. Just then, Tertu barged in. Chief lunged for his eyeglasses. Anna found herself laughing, really laughing, for the first time in days. And that was all.

But Aunt Ethel was talking about more than eyeglasses and mashed potatoes. "I've said more than I should," she repeated. "It's hard here. In the winter I have my ladies—faculty wives. But here everybody's so busy, so wrapped up in this group thing."

Anna found herself staring at the door.

"I know you've got to get back to your children. Don't let me stop you. It was nice, Anna. A little heart-to-heart talk."

Did I talk? Anna wondered.

In her spare moments, Anna watched the students grow up. They were growing up so rapidly, all except for Naomi. Anna watched with prescience; it made her feel her age, seeing so clearly what was to come.

Naomi was the youngest, wide-eyed, still in her milk teeth as far as knowing what the score was. She was bustling with business, all clipboard and caliper, while Joel lurked in the shadows, biding his time, waiting for his moment. The girl wore her hair in a ponytail and kept it tied back with a shoelace or a bit of colored string. Ridiculous habit, really. Joel would snatch the things and run off with them. He slept in a room with a double-decker bed, in the lower bunk and, according to Aunt Ethel, he'd tied a shoelace to each of the springs of Isaiah's bunk overhead, so it looked like a hanging garden. Aunt Ethel felt it incumbent upon her to call Joel in for a lecture on "fetishes." The shoelaces went away, and Joel was transferred to the upper bunk, Isaiah below, to prevent a relapse.

The real trouble was that nobody, but nobody, in that madhouse had any sense of humor.

There were only two blessings on the premises as far as Anna was concerned. It took her some time to realize that they were indeed blessings.

One was a man named Bart—he never told his last name. Anna was standing on the back porch when she first noticed him. He was sitting at a distance, cross-legged on a high ledge, waving a coil of something, oarweed or sea tangle, in the air. It looked like an umbilicus and he seemed to be chanting into the wind.

Artist, she thought. But where were his paints? He didn't even have a sketch pad. Drifter, more likely, some sort of stray. He wore ragpicker togs, a sort of derelict chic: worn denim jacket, embroidered shirt, jeans patched and faded, peon sandals. There was a beaded bag on the ledge beside him, and a hat of wilted suede.

Anna steered a wide path around him, but Jim and Sue were bolder.

Some days at low tide, when the rocks showed their

hair, Anna took the children down to the bluffs to hunt for tidal pools. In these clear but brackish waters, often a foot deep, they poked around for sea anemone, crumb-of-bread sponge, periwinkle and starfish, the soft coral called "sea finger," and limpets in tiny pointed shells the children called "Chinaman's hats."

Next time Anna spotted Bart, he was deep in conversation with Jim. Sue was standing alongside, her eyes riveted on the stranger. It was lasting too long. Anna wasn't eager to interfere but felt she had better find out what was going on.

"Hope they're not pestering you."

"Oh, no, they're nice kids. Full of perk. I don't mind. Used to be that age, myself."

"Not too long ago, I'd say," Anna was quick to put in.

"Quite a ways back, I've done some hard traveling since. Hey, I'm not trespassing or anything, am I? I heard someplace that the land left between high tide and low was no man's, no man could own it. Just like you can't own the sea, no property there. Rights of passage, that's all."

"Sounds right—about the land left by the tide. But don't ask me. I don't own the place."

It was hard to guess his age. He had long disorderly hair, a balding forehead and a full beard, darker than his hair. His eyes were blue, clear and mild.

"What kind of place is this?"

"It's a school."

"Neat. I sure wouldn't mind going to school here. Wouldn't mind owning this view. Funny how nobody here seems to appreciate it. Like, I mean, the students don't get out much."

He slung the bead bag over his shoulder. Then he extracted a tiny notepad, a pencil. He began to jot something down.

"What do they call this school?"

"Four Winds."

"Four Winds? Funny name for a school, isn't it? Sounds like a restaurant or a schooner. An airline, maybe. Scandinavian airlines, that's it."

"This house was around long before any airlines. Well . . . bye, now. I hope my children didn't bother you too much."

"They sure asked a lot of questions, but I don't mind. Like what was I doing out in such a wind yesterday. I didn't mind telling them, I don't mind telling you. 'I'm calming the sea,' I told them. 'I take her when she's fuming and when I am. Making her calm, I calm myself. The word 'Om' helps a lot. I told them to practice it, breathing out slowly. Breathing is so important. If you hear them practicing, I'm the one who started it. They thought it was a pretty funny word, they made it sound like 'OOOM'—you know—the sea booming. A pretty scary sound. Hope you don't mind. I didn't start the Om business, you know. Lots of people noticed it before me.

"There's a chant that really helps. *Rig-Veda*, I think, but I'm no scholar. 'Darkness there was, hidden by darkness, in the beginning. An undistinguished ocean was This All.' Wish I knew Sanskrit. I bet that sounds *fantastic* in Sanskrit! But it even works in English, it really helps.

When I feel all this swarming in me, it helps thinking of how things were, you know, in the beginning before anything was. 'Non-existent there was not. Existent there was not then. There was not the atmospheric space, nor the vault beyond. What stirred where, and in whose control? Was there water, a deep abyss?' Doesn't that blow your mind?"

"Well . . ." Anna began inching off.

"Today really wasn't so good. Dunno why. Sea too quiet maybe. I like it on a day when things are really kicking up."

Harmless, Anna decided, but quite quite mad. As mad as any of the inhabitants of the Four Winds.

The children were already making their way back to the house.

"Gotta go." Anna waved. "See you around. Or if I don't—lotsa luck."

But if Bart heard, he didn't register. She could still hear him when she reached the porch. " 'With eyes and face in all directions . . . with arms and feet in all directions . . .' "

He disappeared for more than a week, then showed up again on the first day of rain and mist. He was wearing a dark poncho and a fisherman's yellow hood.

Anna looked for him whenever the weather was blowing. A calming presence. He rarely missed a storm. Once, his back to her, he waved without turning round.

The other blessing was Isaiah. Every evening between nine and ten, during the social hour, he would bundle up and go out into the garden with his fiddle. She knew he'd been forbidden to practice in the house.

Strange, how the defiant music moved her. Unmusical me, Anna marveled, my ear a bowl and wooden clapper. At concerts, she'd shift in her metal chair. But at the Four Winds it was another story.

One night, tired, aching for sleep, yet knowing she wouldn't fall off until Bob came up, Anna sat on the windowsill. First she heard a plucking and scraping, then warm-ups, then he began—

At the end there was something very slow and tender, a lullaby of sorts. Anna sat on the sill between the window and curtain, half facing in, half out. There was a mild draft from the window. She had turned off the lights in the room and was feeling completely relaxed. Her hands were pressed together: palm matched to palm, shaping a pod in the middle, enclosing emptiness. Long after the music ceased, it hung upon the air. Anna sat motionless, aware of her breathing. Om . . . she said to herself, that's what it must feel like. A dog barked nearby, the motor of a car gunned somewhere in the middle distance, but the lullaby still hung upon the air, hung and spread in widening circles.

Nothing divided her from the night. She thought of the roses blooming on in the deserted garden. They ought to shut fast when the sun goes down, she thought, it's simple prudence.

It cheered her, knowing that they did not.

19

NAOMI HAD RUN into difficulties with her culture medium. She had substituted synthetic agar for plasma as a substratum for the growing tissues. Plasma brought in too many variables, depending on when it was taken, even how it was taken. She concocted a mixture of serum, embryonic tissue extract, Noble agar, and Earle's solution, but found it too concentrated and, in her third attempt, added distilled water, diluting everything by half.

During that difficult week, Lebret teased her by asking how her "cooking" was coming. He favored one particular recipe; it came from the witches in *Macbeth*. "You know how that goes . . ." She wasn't sure, so he recited it for her: " 'In the cauldron boil and bake, eye of newt and toe of frog, wool of bat and tongue of dog, adder's fork and blind-worm's sting . . .' " It was a fact, he told her, that clotted lymph from a frog was the first nutrient ever used in tissue culture.

Finally Naomi was ready to move ahead. She prepared

the tissue explants and inserted them on top of the culturing medium in watch glasses. She set up a few cultures with a supernatant serum layer to see how that would go. She was hoping for the best but not feeling terribly confident.

Her second special project, the one with a strain of genetically obese mice, was not yet under way. But soon would be.

Naomi was walking back from Spemann Lab with Joel, not along the road as they'd been specifically instructed, but taking a cut through the woods. They were talking about the obese mice. The students had seen them for the first time that morning. Naomi was quite excited, since so little was known about the strain. Together with Polly, she'd planned an investigation of their eating habits to find out whether there were any patterns, any regulators of intake.

The obese mice were very expensive, about ten dollars a head, since they were sterile and scarce. You had to breed around them. They were surprisingly attractive with their sleek coats of glossy hair and so many of them piebald. Joel agreed they were "cute," and added that he thought Naomi was "even cuter." Naomi changed the subject. Joel predicted that in five years Naomi would have her M.R.S. Fool that she was, Naomi asked what sort of degree that was—master of what science? Joel blushed for her ignorance. Then she realized. She primly replied that she had no room for marriage in her plans. As far as she was concerned, marriage was best portrayed in some dumb operetta she'd once heard, a forever-after of picking each other's teeth after dining together. Who needed it? No thanks: she wanted to *do* things. Joel said, "Wait and see," looking very smug. Without any kind of warning, he pushed in front of her, grabbed her where she was, and forced his tongue into her mouth. Just like that. This grainy, muscular, fibrillating heap.

Crazy!

She was so surprised. It was far from pleasant. It tasted remotely of rhubarb and unsettled milk. What now? She guessed she was supposed to swoon. Or at least close her eyes. Her lids locked open. Kissing, she watched Joel's eyes collide. Stood horrified, intent on the eye in the middle of his forehead. Stood numb and dumb, with two tongues in her mouth. Two tongues, one eye.

He wriggled.

Behind Joel stood a sumac tree, looking as sumacs always did, dusty and depleted. They separated. Lip broke from lip with a loud report. Joel sailed backwards into the tree.

But didn't seem to mind. He smiled this dizzy smile.

Naomi didn't feel at all romantic. Her first kiss—could that be it? A thing much, much overrated. Maybe he was nervous and didn't do it right. It was a shock, really.

After they detached themselves, they stood awkwardly for a moment. Then Joel took Naomi's hand in his as if they'd agreed on something. What could it be? She'd completely lost the drift of whatever it was they'd been talking about before. They went on walking rapidly, saying nothing. Joel began to whistle, no particular tune. He kept giving her hand these hard, meaningful squeezes, some short, some long, a sort of Morse code. Naomi wondered whether he was nervous. She wanted to ask whether it was the first time for him too. But supposing it wasn't? Chances were, it wasn't the first time for him. Joel was a full seventeen. Naomi decided he must be an old hand at this. She didn't say a word all the way back, not even goodbye when they dropped hands at the gate of the Four Winds.

She took a long look at Joel when they let go. Although she'd been with him every day, she'd never taken the time to notice him before; he'd been little more than a chattering head propped up on the usual substructure. And now? He hadn't suddenly become tall, dark and handsome—the change was more magical than that: a plaster block taking on human shape, color, unique color, living warmth. She noticed how fair he was, and how lavishly freckled. Like an overripe banana, she thought. His hair was sand-colored, close-cropped and very curly. Eyes, nose, mouth—all in the usual places. He was reasonably tall, at least a head taller than she was, though you'd never know it; he didn't use his height to any advantage, hunching most of the time.

That evening Naomi took pains to avoid Joel at supper. She had a report on one of her Basics to write up and she needed time to sort things out. She felt her blood buzzing all over the place, but had nothing so shapely as a thought in her head. Although the experience had been far from pleasant, she felt a distinct triumph afterwards. Sweet sixteen and never been kissed—kids used to say it as a taunt. But it wouldn't apply to her, no, not to her, she'd made it smoothly with a year to spare.

Was this what the girls at school meant when they said "French kiss"? No one had explained these things to her, and Naomi would never have asked. She always acted as if she knew everything there was to know about sex—no voodoo, please. It was all a matter of ducts and ductless glands.

Although people kept telling her she was so advanced for her age, the truth was, Naomi reflected, she wasn't really. Her mother had known this all along. Naomi was far advanced on animals. That's how she'd won her science foundation grant. Her prize project and essay had been on the role of olfaction in guinea pig reproduction. But really, she thought, I'm sadly behind on people.

That night Naomi lay awake trying to remember every detail of the incident in the woods, trying to bind up each incidental twig and leaf and hair. The drab and dusty sumac at Joel's back had become lustrous, radiant oils in the leaves; the sky beyond—a brimming bowl. It seemed forever when she dwelled upon it, and yet it was all over so fast—a minute, not more. Would it have made a difference if she'd known what was coming?

Busy perfecting it, Naomi went over and over the same ground, rehearsing the moment of impact, trying to prepare for it in retrospect, trying somehow to encompass the fact of change. Yesterday I was a child. Today I am an experienced woman.

Yesterday she'd been snug, snug as an unopened bud. Yesterday she'd known who she was and liked herself pretty much as she was.

But now—

She played the scene over from every seat in the house, prompter's box, balcony, dress circle, stage center. It was the same hoarding she'd done as a small child. She used to gather her cut hair, the spilled bangs and ragged ends, stowing them in paper bags in the closet and keeping strict count of her hoardings. Until she moved, and the bag was lost in transit. And she'd collected all her nail clippings in a treasure box, crying if she missed a one; it was the only way she knew of keeping herself together, of containing the changes.

The hours passed. Naomi listened to the television droning away on the floor beneath. She watched the morning come.

Between sunrise and the first bell, she must have napped. The third bell was chiming when Naomi opened her eyes next; Polly was already at the door, about to go on down. Naomi had a thick headache. Had someone clobbered her in her sleep? She was feeling oddly cheerful for such a headache. Twice she caught herself smiling her best social smile at the wall, like a cheap drunk.

Then she remembered. Thinking about it, the morning after, that sour, shapeless kiss had become something else entirely. She left the room, her bed unmade. At the other end of the hallway a door was singing. She negotiated the stairs gingerly, step by single step, jolting to a halt between landings. It occurred to Naomi that she hadn't the faintest idea what to expect next. What was the normal progression from here?

She didn't know. She wasn't ready to know. It was all she could manage to cope with the work before her. An M.R.S. had no place in any of her plans, nor did falling in love—she had no intention of "falling" into anything. Besides—Joel had his hands full with his own projects. They would have to talk things over.

But there was no time for talk. She was late for breakfast and only managed to snatch some cold toast. Then on to floor-scrubbing crew.

Joel caught up with her in the Mouse House. She was busy with her seventh Basic, checking some mice for vaginal plugs, the first sign of conception. There was no one else around.

It was the same kind of kiss. Naomi hadn't thought to put down her probe, and held one arm stiffly extended behind Joel's back so as not to prod or puncture him. This time she knew what was coming. She closed her eyes to see if it was better this way. Their tongues crossed. She explored the subtle facets of his upper palate. Somehow he managed to scrunch his long body up against her. She didn't feel any more romantic, only ticklish to the point of pain, and then hollow—blasted. She was about to break away to start a discussion with Joel about slowing down, when they were both startled by the clanging of a bell. Before eleven: it wasn't any of the scheduled bells. Well-conditioned, they dropped everything and made it up to the house on the double.

A meeting was already in session in the common room. It turned out to be a series of reprimands rather than a meeting. In fact, it was nothing but nags. By the time it was over, romance was worlds away.

Most of the reprimands, it turned out, were directed at a single person, although names were not named and complaints were generalized as "fair warning to all." If Isaiah hadn't jumped into the fray as usual, it might have escaped notice that so many of the warnings were directed at him.

Chief announced that lab doors were to be kept open at all times. When Isaiah raised his hand to put a word in, heads turned; this wasn't intended to be a debate. There was too much noise, Isaiah claimed, he had to close his door to concentrate.

Too bad, said Chief; scientists have to learn to concentrate in labs with plenty of people and lots of noise.

The full story emerged later: a great fuss over a single incident. The evening before, without a knock or any kind of warning signal, Isaiah's lab door burst open. He jumped —as who wouldn't? He was visibly shaken. It was Aunt Ethel. "Who did you think it would be," she greeted him, "the Dew Fairy?"

On to the subject of black marks. Aunt Ethel was keeping a ledger. Successful completion of the summer program would depend upon all-round performance. Housework was not the least factor in this average. Lest they forget, the Four Winds belonged to the students on trust. For the sake of future generations of students, they would have to take care of it.

Isaiah buttonholed Joel after the meeting to fill him in on the details. Only an hour before, he'd been called down to the small dining room, and his personal page in Aunt Ethel's black book had been shown to him. The comments margin was full of his sins: not socializing, sloppy housework, practicing his violin when expressly forbidden to, and making snide remarks about an electrical extension. "What kind of remarks about *what?*" Isaiah had cried out. Hadn't Isaiah asked for an electrical extension? Yes, he'd asked for an extension the week before but hadn't yet received it. When Chief asked why Isaiah and

Joel weren't both using their gooseneck lamps, Isaiah had explained that, because Aunt Ethel was busy, he hadn't yet gotten his extension. Chief had called that "a nasty dig."

Isaiah was told to socialize more, to start being a help on work crew, and to keep a smile on his face. "What a farce," Isaiah snapped. "Whenever I smile, I'm told to wipe the smirk off my face—so what am I to do?" Housework was no laughing matter, although Isaiah plainly thought otherwise. Tidiness and cleanliness were of first importance in the summer program. First importance to whom? Isaiah didn't dare ask. But to Joel, he spelled it out: "To Aunt Ethel, of course. Little islands of order in a raging sea." Chief took Isaiah aside afterwards and told him that this was "the third warning." The first warning had come after the collision on the stairs, the second after he'd persisted in practicing on the lawn.

Chief didn't specify how many warnings he had to go.

After he was finished with Joel, Isaiah went over the same details with Naomi. Naomi found it hard to be as sympathetic as she might have been. She couldn't help thinking that Isaiah enjoyed the struggle, just a little bit. Also, she had to look out for herself.

"Why are you forcing Aunt Ethel's hand? While you're here, why not make the best of it? Play the game, follow the rules." Naomi was amazed to hear herself: she sounded like her own mother. But, clearly, there were limits beyond which resistance defeated itself.

"What is the game? What *are* the rules? You'd think I robbed that woman of the air she breathes, she hates me so much."

To Isaiah, Aunt Ethel was "a raging sea"; to Naomi, she seemed all bottled up. Were they talking about the same person? How could both be true?

Aunt Ethel was deeply troubled about something or someone. That much was obvious, but who or what it was, no one could say. She'd been wearing the same rumpled denims for days, her white blouse had grown yellow in the collar and around the armpits; she seemed too preoccupied to notice.

Except for the organization and supervision of work crews, there were days when Aunt Ethel didn't show her face. Not that they didn't feel her presence. Most of the students had the feeling that the Four Winds was her home and that they were houseguests, there by the grace of her personal invitation. And only so long as she suffered them to be there. Naomi, for one, felt Aunt Ethel was everywhere present, even when hidden away in her room. She could hear the television going many hours a day and nearly all through the night.

These nightly television marathons were a new development. Was Aunt Ethel having some sort of trouble sleeping? Naomi was, and that was how she came to hear late shows and late late shows, laughter, sobs, voices shifting, curtain music, the refrain "stay tuned!"; dawning suspense, dire warning, detergent interludes, "stay tuned!"; the heavy chords of catastrophe, goodbye forever, clinching embrace, happy ending, tragic ending, stay tuned, stay tuned . . .

When Aunt Ethel came down for breakfast after her long night, she was terrible to behold. The whites of her eyes were rusted and her face was scarred with living

149

through so many emotions and disasters. She would check up on each of the housekeeping crews; then, after she was sure that cleaning operations were in full swing, she'd disappear, sometimes until evening. Sometimes they wouldn't see her again until supper came around.

20

I can hardly remember the sun. The fog is unrelieved. Seems hard to believe we've had only two days of it. This is only the third day. But it's so pervasive, it's as if nothing else ever was. The damp clings. There's a dull pewter light over everything. The red in Mr. Homay's lumber jacket and the least of colors in the garden seem on fire by contrast. Four Winds is islanded in mist and things seem more dreamed than real. Land is cut off from sea. Treetop and hilltop dissolve in mid-height. To the animals in the grass, I must seem headless, too.

We can only guess the nearness of the ocean. There's something out there, some seething cauldron. We hear the vast smother and spill, and gauge the immensity we can no longer see. The foghorn of a boat blares through—lost. I only hope the coast guard is listening. No one here is. We are wrapped in our own internal mist, web on web. Busy, infernally busy, half blind with being so busy.

My projects are under way. I'm moving on, as blindly as the rest.

Eva— Never mind.

I keep telling them to call me Jerry and not to be so formal. But all I ever hear is Jerome. The name must suit me. Jerome-the-dour, the dry-as-dust. Well, aren't I?

People. Chief and Aunt Ethel—alleles.

Isaiah at a lecture. He sits very upright, very rigid, his neck in invisible traction. Face of igneous texture. A cold, unassimilated presence, unassimilable. And a sitting duck as far as Aunt Ethel is concerned. A precise target. Recently she's been confining herself to sniping at his fiddle. This must be a house of the deaf for Isaiah, enough to make any musician tear his hair out. But it isn't really music at issue.

If it wasn't the fiddle, it would be something else—his grooming or accent or the color of his eyes or his manners. Socially, he's a constant source of soreness, heat and friction. He doesn't believe in words as lubricants as the rest of us do— "how nice"—"don't you think?"—"I agree with you there"— words like that. Even when he wants to tell you what he feels he never warms up to the subject or tries to create a climate of reciprocity, he simply blurts out the essential matter, and the rest of us can take it or leave it. Mostly we leave it.

As for his table manners! I'm no paragon but he's downright messy. He eats with two spoons sometimes, shoveling, stooping low over his food. He arranges his string beans in hieroglyphs on the plate. His mind is always elsewhere. He tears his bread to bits and rolls the bits into balls, then lengthens them into pellets with restless fingers. In the end they lie in his plate, gray, like slugs.

But if it wasn't his manners, it would be something else. Any pretext, for Isaiah is the quintessential Jew. I don't mean his religion, since I doubt he has any. He's probably an agnostic or a humanist or an out-and-out atheist—that's not the point. And I certainly don't mean anything racial. The Jews have their Jews.

What I'm thinking of is a purely social syndrome. Wherever he goes, whatever he does, Isaiah stands apart. He's never lost in a crowd. Should he mingle, he'd never blend. Going his own determined way and seeming to need our good opinion so little, he simply invites our envy and scorn. Yet he provokes, God knows he provokes. He will not accommodate. He has his reasons, enough reasons. He will not bend. And he cherishes every blow.

We need him. In some crazy way, we depend on him to do the outrageous thing. He has a way of speaking his mind (our minds). What the rest of us only dare to think silently, he blurts out—top voice. We ought to cherish him. He lets off steam for all of us, a safety valve in this pressure cooker of a house.

I thought it would pass, but Aunt Ethel grows more and more a puzzle every day. Her obsession with cleanliness, for instance—what is it? Her eyes look out from very deeply in. What is it that she sees? Some sad, foul vision of the world as urinal? The waste? An unused woman, I think. Nothing to do. And anyway, the time for doing it is over now. Her bitter leisure is felt all over the house.

More interesting than any of my projects are the people here, the things they do and profess to do, often at cross-purposes. Myself included. I watch myself—pretty thorny. And here the nicest cunning is required, sneak and ambush the only method.

I blush a lot. It can happen merely by thinking about blushing or by someone saying the word "blush." What does it mean? It's not a case of cryptic coloration. It's more self-sabotage than camouflage—a haze upon the unmasking of intention, a red flag of discretion, apology and celebration in one. Not at all clear what purpose it serves or subverts—some social code? I never blush below the neck where it might pass unnoticed. I doubt very much whether anyone else does. It's only a hunch. No hard data. I ought to watch people in bathing suits. Provoke them and watch.

Reminder: WATCH

Must remember. Is blushing involuntary? Not likely, I think. It's so mixed up with propriety and so centered on the face. By blushing we speak, that's my guess. We speak—though grammar and logic escape me. A kind of double-speak—yes and no at the same instant, both emphatically.

That's the human. The hyphenated, the blushing beast. Angelic beast, bestial angel. Where the Alkahest would erect a shrine—I tremble.

21

It was so quiet Anna could hear the two-way radios of the fishermen, cackling like geese, blabbing over the waters. Island news, depth soundings, harbor gossip, obscenities. Red-eyed with sun and solitude, they sounded, circling round, slowly going crackers.

Such a nothing day. She could even hear the clocks in the Four Winds, and her own heart. Time, the nibbler. Anna recalled the sign on the rocks at Breaker's Point: "The sea is wearing the land away. Each little wave takes its little toll. The sea has infinite time."

It applied, it applied all too well.

Two o'clock. It was the children's napping hour. The students were busy on their own. Bob Homay had picked up a gallon thermos jug in town. He wanted to fill it with ice and fruit punch and present it as a surprise to Anna. There were gallons and gallons of juice in the kitchen—

why shouldn't his family be entitled to a little? It would be only fair, considering all the extra work they did. At the same time, Bob didn't know whether this borrowing was legal or not; he supposed it wasn't. So he stepped softly, crossing the threshold of the kitchen.

All quiet.

The students were in the Mouse House, counting out their red blood cells, their white blood cells, their platelets, their reticulocytes, their tumor transplants and vaginal plugs, infarctions, furuncles, fibroses, pustules and polyps—they did a lot of counting.

From the cupboard there came a rapid thumping, clotted speech. Someone was saying "Don't, please! Don't." Again and again. A woman's voice, sounding as though she were being throttled.

The door of the cupboard was slightly ajar. Bob applied his eye to it. He was treated to a slice of Doris, her skirt caught on something—some sacks and barrels stood in the way. No, they didn't. The arm of a white jacket flashed upwards, a crest of graying hair, a long back—Chief! He was feeling the lady up and down, but she was making no sound at all now. If she didn't like it, she wasn't saying. Bob didn't wait to see more. He slammed the door hard behind him.

They must have heard. There were cries within.

Upstairs, Anna was laying out tools, getting ready to do her eyebrows and fingernails. Bob came sprinting up the stairs with a red face and a present, which he thrust at her.

Anna was delighted with the jug until she discovered it was empty. Bob didn't want to explain. "Let's take a short nap," he whispered, "how about it? I'm feeling frisky." He gave her a squeeze and a wink that she supposed he supposed was sexy.

"You're changing the subject, Bob. Nap? At this hour? What can you be thinking of? The children will be stirring any minute now. Didn't you think of picking up a can of juice while you were at the store? Why not? A little common sense."

"And why should I pay for juice? Room and board, they promised us. Remember that brochure? Help yourself to some juice in the kitchen when the kids get up. After all, we work for our keep." Bob raised his voice with more belligerence than Anna thought the situation warranted. If he had started out the summer with that much self-assertion, their situation might have been different; by now it was too late.

"And anyway," he added, "isn't Tertu a friend of yours?"

"Friend or no friend, there's only one person who counts around here—her name isn't Tertu. And she isn't much of a friend. Nice thought, anyway. Kitchen is strictly out of bounds between mealtimes. Thought you knew the rules."

Bob shrugged his shoulders, said he didn't want to quarrel, and muttered something incoherent about counting her blessings. "What does *that* mean?" Anna wanted to know.

But he walked off abruptly without explaining further.

"Do you love your husband as I do mine?" Anna found herself echoing Aunt Ethel's question from time to time. She was certain that she didn't, and that it was just as well. Aunt Ethel's love was a heavy affliction—who needed it? It gave no one joy or peace.

Anna had once loved like that. A struggling poet named Michael. He was "all temperament" and seemed to inhabit a turbulent world made entirely of liquids, where passion followed passion, continually canceling and supplanting what went before so that nothing fixed or solid remained.

"I caught you in one of the sadder flights of my fancy," he'd written in one of his most melancholy letters. It arrived two days after a perfectly happy meeting.

His letters to her were all bravura pieces. The transience of spring, lengthening shadows, sunset, the rain, somehow he managed to bring it all in. Anna and Michael had lasted three seasons together and each day had brought a fresh simile and an extended theme. In the end it was wearing.

Anna had married not long after their break, to a man as unlike Michael as possible. "On the rebound," her friends said. Maybe so, but in many ways Anna had known what she was doing. Bob was a ballast—he balanced her. A dull man, yes, but also, in his own stubborn, ineffectual, bumbling way, essentially sound, a good man.

He was also, at times, her most incorrigible child.

Jim and Susie had been good all day. After they finished their naps, Anna made the mistake of telling them so. Jim said: "Why is being good so boring?" and began to look for something less boring to do. Give him a few minutes and he'd find it.

Lately the children had begun pestering Anna about television. They wanted to know why they couldn't watch, since by now they were well aware that there was a set in the house. "You get enough TV at home. Far too much of it," Anna said firmly. "I want you to make the most of the summer. The beautiful outdoors."

Jim was quick to catch the contradiction: "We aren't outdoors all the time. We stay in the room a lot! Like right now. When it rains. And when it fogs up. Like when we had all those foggy days. It's not fair." At this point, Sue chimed in: "Aunt Ethel doesn't share. It isn't nice to hog, you said so. *She* hogs."

"Well," Anna conceded, "Aunt Ethel has her problems. Anyhow, she's grown up, so there's nothing any of us can do about it."

Anna propped up her magnifying mirror at an angle to the window and studied her face. A sieve, she saw. She swung the mirror around to the non-magnifying side. Better that way. The face was familiar.

She noticed lines, the first tentative strokes between the eyebrows. The lifts of her smile stood out sharply. She saw herself in age, her face stamped with a trident. That would come first. Then later, even the stamp would splinter, the features swim apart. Time: a rake with teeth evenly spaced.

Oh, to get back to that first freshness! If only she could look at green hills without thinking of mentholated anything. Anna selected her delicate splinter tweezers and began plucking the finer hairs between her eyebrows, an operation that never failed to make her wince. Then she took out the heavier tweezers and began shaping.

The trouble was that one eyebrow always turned out higher than the other, giving her face an insinuating look, an eyebrow always raised. She couldn't really remember how the true line went—arch? angle? quaver? Ought to rescue an old photo, she decided, way back when. When? When she was eleven? Twelve? At the business of dissemblance even then? What was the true line? What did my eyes say? she wondered.

She gave a little snort—here she was in one of the most enlightened scientific institutions in the world, living the life of an unofficial mouse. She could write it up, this summer, this "summer of the mind," as Dr. Alkavist liked to call it, his pioneering educational experiment. Title: *Thoughts from Purdah—or—Life from Under the Tablecloth.* Or, better still: *Confessions of an After-Dinner Mint.* Yes, she ought. Plucking, Anna paused. The children were awfully quiet. Go and see? No—no need.

"There's nothing to do," Jim began. "We've read all the comics."

"I've got a magazine with pictures," Anna offered. "Why don't you two settle down on the bed with it?"

They read the glossy ads. "Mommy, is that real?" Susie droned after every page. "Or is it just pretend?" Anna didn't bother to examine the page after the third question. "Pretend," she answered. "They're all pretend people, baking pretend cookies, making pretend phone calls, playing pretend chess, painting pretend paintings, kissing pretend kisses. It's all pretend."

"Is this a pretend school?" Susie asked, looking up.

"You mean the Four Winds? Oh, no, this is for real."

Anna had started having visitors from time to time, refugees from what had come to be called "the lower house." There was Ao, the cat, for one. "Visitor" was not the scrupulously correct word: Ao was more of a conscripted guest. The children had a habit of borrowing her, coaxing her up the steps with a rag or a spool. But no one seemed to notice, let alone object.

Isaiah was another frequent visitor. He'd knock and enter at once, without any ceremonial interlude. He never asked if he might be interrupting something. And he showed up on the slightest pretext or no pretext at all. One day he noticed Ao playing in the doorway and followed her inside without knocking, without so much as "Hi."

"A cat's mind is her nose," he observed by way of greeting, "know what I mean?" He tried to be chummy with Jim and Susie, but they didn't like him and showed they didn't by running off in the middle of his discussions. Sue said in private: "His face is all bumpy. And he talks sideways." Anna tried her best to like him, but it wasn't easy. Often, the closest she could come was to feel sorry for him. Lately she noticed dirty circles under his eyes—

lack of sleep, unclean habits, anyone's guess. He hung around, seeking some sort of comfort. But how did you comfort someone who'd outgrown stuffed dolls and lollies, mother comfort, who'd gone beyond all that?

He didn't seem to be practicing much in the evenings now. He'd made some attempts to socialize with the other students, but without success, lacking some skill that everyone else took for granted. Maybe not so much a missing skill as a lack of casualness. He stood apart from everyone. It was something almost physical, so clearly marked. He wore his sense of difference like a caul. It wasn't that he didn't try, perhaps he tried too hard. Anna overheard him making overtures to Naomi.

"At home right now I'd be tying the curtains up in knots to let some breeze in. Guess I'm a little homesick. Aren't you?"

"Too busy, Isaiah. I really don't think about it."

"Sometimes I think I'd rather be in New York, breathing in little nuggets of hell, than here."

"Not me. I like the country air."

Goose! As if they were talking about air!

"Tell you what I do like," Isaiah conceded. "When I sit alone in my lab and look outside at the ocean. It's a high window over the world."

That evening Isaiah came out to the back porch where Anna and the children were sitting. He perched on the rail as though he were studying the view and waited for Anna to say something.

"Why aren't you practicing? I miss my evening concert."

"*Verboten*, haven't you heard?"

"That never stopped you before."

"I thought I'd hang by my thumbs for my music if it came to that. Now I'm not sure I'd hang by my thumbs for anything at all. Sad, isn't it? Everybody keeps saying these are the best years, being young and all. If these are the best, I can't imagine what the not-so-good, or the worst, what the worst will be like. I'm so miserable now."

"You make yourself miserable," said Anna, not really listening, only enough to pick up the familiar tone of lamentation. She was trying to extricate the comb from Susie's hair. A nest of snags: she'd have to work through it slowly with brush and fingers.

"Why does everybody hate me?" he continued.

"That's not true."

"It is—I can tell. I get the feeling everybody wishes I'd just evaporate. Maybe someday I will."

"You give yourself too much importance. Most people are indifferent. You're part of the background as far as they're concerned. Everyone's foreground is himself."

"Aunt Ethel is *not* indifferent," he contradicted sharply. "And she's about as subtle as Cinerama about how she feels. Take my word for it. The vials of wrath are ready to be poured out. In glorious technicolor and 3-D! Just you wait and see. It's like she'd given me a blown-bridge problem."

"A what?"

"It's a stress experiment. You can do it to a group, or

single someone out. Let's say you single someone out. You order him to build a bridge. But the planks you give him for material are either too short or too few. A loaded situation, see? Only what makes it real hell is that the test subject, the target person—he doesn't know it's loaded."

"I see." Anna didn't—quite.

There was a pause and she thought now he'd got that out of his system. But no, no such luck. He was still going strong.

"I feel so cut off from this group thing."

"You *are* cut off. But you deliberately make yourself more separate than you have to be," Anna said in a burst. This "group thing"—what is it? she wondered. Same words Aunt Ethel used. All I see is a crowd of separate people. Only thing that brings us together is the bells, that's why they ring so often. Call this a group? We're all cut off, Anna thought. Take a look at me, take a good look at Aunt Ethel—think she's part of anything? More like that old woman she'd seen once in Montreal, hobbling from phone booth to phone booth, shouting into the receivers: "I told you to stop calling me!" But no one was calling her. That was the problem.

Another tangle: Anna continued working the comb through Susie's hair. The rain had stopped. A white-throated sparrow passed by. He sounded no different from the white-throated sparrows they had at home. At home, they were supposed to sing "sweet, sweet, sweet Canada," but here it was supposed to be "old Sam Peabody, old, old." That was what the bird books said, anyhow. To Anna, it seemed the same two words always: "You—me me me me . . ."

Isaiah was talking on and on. Anna couldn't hear herself think. The boy was too bright for her. He talked too fast. When he got excited, she tended to focus on his acne or at the place where his chin was red and chapped from the fiddle. Funny how, even when he wasn't practicing, the mark remained.

She couldn't think at all. Sorry to disappoint. Very high, high flown conversation. Something about wars being due to (who knew how they got into it?) the fixity of relational filters or rigidities of perception and the essential question being how to dismantle the poison-gas factories without being dismantled yourself. Something like that. Anna was still finding snags in Sue's hair, the white-throated sparrow was harping and harping, and she couldn't make head or tail of what the boy was saying. One of the hardships in talking with Isaiah was that, whenever he grew especially serious, he mispronounced so many words, the wrong emphasis on the wrong syllable, which left the listener lagging and guessing. Anna could tell that he had never heard these words spoken, he'd only read them, and it didn't take much to infer that there was no one in his family or among his classmates who used such words. You could tell he was alone.

In spite of the best will in the world, Anna found Isaiah more than usually taxing that evening. She was sick of staring at his acne, for one thing. And she was dumbfounded, simply dumbfounded, at his torrent of words. Whatever it was—feeling she'd failed him, failed even to make an effort to understand him, she decided not to do the thing by halves, and she failed him good and proper. The demands he made upon people were too much, really way over. Yes, he had a lot of growing up to do. Anna told him he ought to be mixing with the other students. "What you're saying is nothing, nothing but words," she blurted out, "a shower solo, a shaving speech. Talk to your mirror like that!" It was the children distracting her so she couldn't listen; she hadn't meant to sound so harsh. Sue was rolling the dirt between her toes, the stuff she called "toe jam," and Jim was carefully picking his nose; they had turned to their own resources, having exhausted toys. These little masturbatory diversions drove Anna up the wall.

"My God, Isaiah," she declared with more vehemence than she intended, "real life! Will you ever catch up with it?"

He turned away without another word.

22

"HAVE A SEAT, ANNA."

Anna took a chair facing Aunt Ethel. She'd been called into the Eloson's private dining room early that morning. Something was up, but Anna was in no hurry to find out what.

Aunt Ethel was wearing a green satin dressing gown. It was brilliantly colored with parrots and flamingos. Her face, in contrast, was pale and raddled. She propped her head on her hands as if it were very heavy.

"Had breakfast?"

Anna nodded.

"Enough?" She tapped the plate of doughnuts in front of her.

"Got to watch my figure," Anna said. "Thanks anyway."

Aunt Ethel continued sipping coffee for a few minutes in silence. She emptied the cup; she studied the bottom of the cup. She weighed the hollow, she swished the emptiness around; she pushed the cup away. She crossed her legs and dangled her slipper on the high foot.

Then she lit up, shaking the match and frowning. "How I hate this habit!"

"Ever try to give it up?"

"Have I? If I tried once, I tried a hundred times! Never worked out. I can't stand the taste of my own mouth, to tell the truth. It tastes like a railroad tunnel. Like death. So here I am killing myself trying to get that taste out, lot of sense it makes. Anyhow, that's my problem. It was something else I wanted to talk to you about. I think you should know that I'm putting Isaiah on probation."

"But why?" Anna replied.

"Why?" Her slipper clattered to the ground, her voice rose. "*Why?*" There was a pause and a scuffle as she hooked the slipper with her big toe. Then she settled both feet, soles flat on the ground. "Hasn't Bob said anything at all to you? You coddle Isaiah. You do, Anna. I've noticed. I know he's got everybody suffering for him."

"Is that why you're putting him on probation? Because we all suffer for him?"

"That's not fair, Anna. You know the reasons as well as I."

"He's different—that's obvious," said Anna. "He's an artist."

"Maybe he is an artist," Aunt Ethel granted doubtfully, "maybe so. But that doesn't excuse anything."

"He's stubborn," Anna suggested.

"He's rude. And he whines so. What does he think life is—a layer cake? Everlasting gum? What does he have to complain about? I'd like to know. Really, I'd like to know. He's young, everything going for him. Everything easy for him, too easy maybe. Is he grateful, the least bit grateful for the opportunity he has here? It's the chance of a lifetime. Does he respect this beautiful house? You know what he says to me? He—"

"But does it matter what he says?" Anna broke in with some heat. The force of her own emotion surprised her. It was far easier to plead for the boy than to actually bear with him. And she was aware of a strange doubleness in herself as she said again: "Does it really matter what he says? Surely you can hear the echoes of his voice? How alone he feels. He's so bright. You can't deny he's bright."

"Bright, why sure, they're *all* bright, Anna. He doesn't fit in somehow. Scatterbrained . . . I don't know . . . too many interests. Something."

"He's not like the others," Anna said again.

"If he wanted music, what's he doing here? Hm? Let me tell you something, Anna. I once wanted a piano. I wanted it more than anything in the world. I grew out of it—I had to. Nobody was going to buy me a piano. First things first. First work, then play. Comes a certain time, you put away toys. Everybody has to give up something. I worked right through high school, at the cleaner's, five-and-dime, you name it. I swept floors in a beauty parlor. Think anybody asked me what my feelings were? By the time I could afford a piano, I was putting Frank through medical school. Fact of life. Adolescents always dream they're great artists because their own feelings move them so. Well, feelings don't count. Sooner he gets to know that, the better off he'll be. The surest path to ruin I know is living by your feelings. Everybody on earth has got them—feelings. You can't run a world by them—"

"To get back to Isaiah—" Anna put in.

"He'll get over it, this music thing. Like I did. Sure it hurts. But he's got to make a living, doesn't he? I'm doing him a favor, setting him straight."

"For being different, you're putting him on probation."

"To teach him a lesson before it's too late. Anyhow, it's a warning, like I said. A warning never hurt anybody. I don't think it will make a bit of difference, frankly. He's got the most stubborn nature. And he's mocking me, Anna. He is, I know it, all the time."

"I'm sure not," Anna protested. She sounded sure.

"He'll take me seriously from now on. I'll make him sit up and take notice."

"You'll give him a chance, then?"

"Oh, sure." She struck a match. "Sure, sure. Well, here's to hoping!" She sat very still for a moment, hands in her lap, the smoke rising and twisting, stinging her eyes. When she began to speak again, it was very softly. "You know, Anna, these are my children. When you can get children to say 'thank you' and mean it, then you've got something. These children are my thank-you-for-living."

"And Isaiah isn't?"

"Isaiah's a pain in the—well, you know where."

"But if you could get him to say 'thank you' and mean it, then you'd really have something, wouldn't you?"

"You know as well as I, that would never happen, he'd never *let* it happen."

Your truest son, thought Anna.

23

THIS WAS HIS DREAM: a car zooming along the thruway. Hilly country. He was looking through the window, enjoying the rush, the sudden rises, sudden falls. He felt free, deliriously free. Leaning back, he studied the shoulder of the driver in front of him—but there was no shoulder. There was no driver, he was alone in the car. The car began to veer over the middle line and he lurched forward, grabbed the steering wheel in the nick of time, but the speed of the vehicle was dizzying, he couldn't connect with the brake—

He'd dreamed that two nights in one week, the same dream with the same payoff, the same vacuous denouement. He'd bolted awake on the brink of disaster each time, shaken, shaken to the core. The dizzying speed, the lurching forward, that was his heart. The dream took him to the brink of knowledge, to the edge, no further.

Dreams . . . Chief shrugged. His dreams didn't help, but they colored his days. These glum skies: were they outside him or within? Sometimes he wasn't sure.

Chief stood on the porch, breathing deeply and nursing a gin and tonic. There'd been an eerie green light in the sky only moments before. When the sun went down over the water's edge, the pines rose and blackened.

There were water sounds, wind sounds, but no voices. The students were in their labs upstairs, most likely; it was an unscheduled time. More than an hour ago Ethel had gone off to town with Tertu. The Homays must be somewhere on the premises, hoping not to be noticed. A happy family, busy with whatever it was that kept happy families busy. Fine with him.

Doris was making herself scarce. He didn't know how she felt about yesterday or if she felt at all. She made a lot of noise at first, then stopped. He'd been going strong when some idiot crashed the door and scared them both out of their wits. His courage had ebbed away after that. He'd give a lot to know who slammed that door. They'd been behind a burlap sack full of flour—chances were, nothing was visible but their heads and shoulders. But he couldn't be sure. If not— Why, I hope you had a feast for the eyes, he whispered to the air. That's more than I got.

He looked out. Last night had been a stormy one. Debris and foam were strewn like garlands over the crest of the Cormorant and the low inshore bluffs.

Suppose he had made it with Doris, she was easy prey, what then? Where would that have gotten him? Hadn't he dallied with a Doris before? He couldn't even remember their names. One so unlikely he called her "the frog." It wasn't swagger, he kept no count of his conquests. He told no tales. He'd taken them all on the same rushing chord. No reason. Or, if there was, it was only to feel alive for a moment. And he had felt alive. For a moment. But none of them mattered. What mattered was the one he never had and never would. He raised his glass.

Closing his eyes, he began to drink with great concentration, his whole body rigid. His lips distended, following the curvature of the glass, glued fast to the rim. He drank to assuage a long thirst, knowing he could not.

His life was much reduced these days. A standard pellet diet and water *ad libitum*. If all the summer had to offer him was the likes of Doris, it would be just that: pellets and water. There were no women around at all. Maybe one or two in town, but he hadn't time to go fishing. Anna Homay had a sweet shape but he'd met her type before: profoundly unavailable, laughing his advances off, not even feeling threatened.

Eva Probst reminded him a little of Fern. It was her coloring, the sheen of her hair, brassy, like band music. Evie had her own style, though. That sweet scent of hers—did they bottle it in Kansas? It surrounded her like a haze, emanations from every pulse point. Silly kid. Who was it for? For him? Not likely. Sweet to have around, anyway. Wore her jeans so tight she'd end up with crotch rot. Hey, none of that. Eva was out of the question; here he stood *in loco parentis*, so hands off.

Shifting his glass, he stretched out first the fingers of one hand, then the other. Powerful fingers, he had, prepotent—ha! "Five lusty pricks," he murmured fervently, "and again five!" The sound of his own voice shocked him. Had he come so far—whispering obscenities to himself? Worse yet, lies. Power? What power? He was pulp, nothing. Swaying with every current. When he should have held fast, he'd let go, his fingers deserted him.

They'd been hiding out in his garage. He'd taken her face in trembling hands, a man whose hands never trembled. Aloha. Moth-soft, her skin. He'd pressed his lips to Fern's as if to slake a thirst. They clung to each other.

The door gave with a grunt, heaving slowly upwards. The light widened: wheels, coil of pipe, prong of rake, blade of hanging shears; the light struck her hair, a blaze of wheat, a shout—

They fell away like puppets, cut down. A figure with no depth, only a pasteboard shadow, was standing in the open door.

Fern had run off to New York. She'd left him a note of two lines: she didn't want to hurt anyone, she hated scenes. He'd rushed after her, too late. He never found her. She'd been Max's student: obstetrics. It had been the middle of the semester; she hadn't finished, and maybe never would now, but not for lack of talent.

In his absence, Ethel had signed him up for another summer at the Four Winds. "Good air up there. Nice scenery. It'll take your mind off things," she explained patiently. "Things!" he cried out. "Take my mind off *things?*"

The Four Winds was nothing but a place of exile for him. It was a good place for Ethel. Gave her something to do. Mistress Manager, she managed everyone. Loading on the guilt. Here, at least, she was off his back. Especially this summer. She had her hands full in any year, but this summer she had Isaiah to contend with. Let her run the place, let her have her fill. There wasn't a spark of interest in it for him. He'd been through it all before: the old director mumbling at the lectern, waving his arms and rattling collection cans. The students might have been pressed from a mold—he'd seen them all before. All but one.

He thought about making a clean break, but knew it would never be clean. He couldn't leave Ethel but, in staying, he didn't really remain; he was always in some other place or time, in memory or anticipation, memory or daydream. His eyes had the enfeebled, bleached look of a dweller in darkness, of a cave creature who did not live in orientation to the present sun but to its after-image.

No, he'd never be able to ditch Ethel. He owed her too much. He owed her everything. Everything said so. Even the waves seemed to murmur: "How much? This much. How much? *So-oh* much," as they came, row on endless row. Someone was adding them up.

She'd bought her way in by supporting him through medical school, but he could not, ever, buy his way out. He'd tried. He'd made good her loan, paid up every penny with interest accruing—her own account to do with as she pleased. She could be comfortably independent if she cared to be. Naturally, she refused to touch her wealth. Her investment in him had not been money; there was no way to equalize the debt. So he stayed on, made a decade of determined efforts, adjustments—one, two, fifty—she loved him, he didn't love her, he needed to love; he stayed on, but refused to embrace his chains.

As for his career, he still went through the motions.

Maybe, someday, he'd make the big breakthrough on lung-transplant technique. But probably not. It made remarkably little difference to him either way. So many imperatives he'd let go. His career didn't amount to a hill of beans, really. He'd never do anything new, not now. He had enough tricks in his repertoire to do something that looked new but wasn't really. Fact was, he reflected, a man pushing fifty has taken his own measure and knows exactly what his mind and skills are worth. He'd rather be admired for the length of his—

His glass was empty—no, there was nearly a drop, and two diminished ice cubes. He shattered a cube between his teeth: the shocks were thrilling. Real, anyway. Isaiah rounded the porch, whistling something fancy. Ethel was wrong there: you couldn't really keep that boy from his music. If you prevented him from whistling, he'd most likely strum the glass with his fingers; if you strapped his hands, he'd drum with his feet. He'd tried to speak to Ethel about Isaiah, but they'd gotten nowhere. To her, playing a fiddle was no innocent business. It could be, she admitted, it could be as innocent as flying a kite or blowing soap bubbles. If you took it up as a pastime, after the world's work was accomplished and all your obligations were met, then that was fine. But it was inexcusable otherwise. Isaiah never pursued his music in the spirit of pastime, and he left most of his obligations unmet. That being so, his music was a serious breach, deeply subversive of order and restraint, a dangerous wallowing in feeling. She'd managed to twist the issue so that they were talking about themselves:

"You're a weak man, Frank. I'm strong. I made myself strong. I had to—to survive. A regular bleeding heart, you are. Except for where your wife's concerned."

She managed to slant every issue.

And that was marriage. He'd traded the risk of happiness with its risk of misery for the dull surety of peace. Not even peace, but this unquiet truce. Minimax. It had dulled him, even his pain was dim. He'd gladly salt his wounds. The years of his domesticity were as a day compared to the lifetime-in-minutes of loving hard, the color and richness and speed. He'd have given anything to recall the pain, the sweet caustic of loss as he touched her face for the first, and last, time. Never before had he felt so stirred, so unholy, so gashed up, so alive.

Only a leaden numbness remained now. He looked up: a lackluster moon shorn of its sex, its beams. Pale satellite. Locked fountain. It spoke to him, one to one. And, on earth, only the crickets were about. Only the crickets, crying out "thirst, thirst," their voices parched and scorched.

Aunt Ethel, entering in silence, studied the back of her husband for some minutes without breaking the spell. Celestial gooseflesh, he had, her husband. Shuddering dewlaps, her stud. (He gazed at the moon, he gazed at his feet, he gazed at the moon again.) He did not turn or notice his wife's coming. She held her breath, so intent you could see the ropes in her neck and a big vein keeping count.

Her husband stood stock still, in the ramrod posture of a man with piles.

He's remembering love, she thought.

Sure enough, he folded his glass in tender hands and clutched it to his chest.

Something rattled.

24

Ten thirty. Naomi had only just settled down to work when the bells began. A regular carillon. Four, five, six—now what?

This time, they gathered in the seminar room. There were quite a few reporters, some from as far away as Boston, busy interviewing the Alkahest and Chief. And a cluster of photographers, one standing on a chair, trying to get some angles on the students. When they learned that Naomi was the youngest, a couple of them asked her to pose separately. They insisted she keep on her lab coat, and set her up pointing to a blackboard full of scrawled abbreviations and formulae, the legacy of some visiting lecturer. Only one phrase stood out: "viable mutants," chalked in big block letters.

The Boston reporters were particularly tough; they interviewed the Alkahest at length, eager for more details of his wife and the history of the Four Winds. But the Alkahest refused to dwell upon the past. They asked him repeatedly how the summer program was funded. He named the national research foundation grants, the specialized institutes and a few of the smaller contributors, inviting anyone interested to inspect his books.

Next the reporters wanted to know his thoughts as a researcher on the connection between cigarette smoking and cancer.

His personal opinion? Obviously, some of his colleagues saw the matter differently. As for himself, the Alkahest said he didn't think much of it. The evidence was only circumstantial so far. For example, no one had yet eliminated the possibility that the complex physiological and personality factors that led people to smoking in the first place weren't the cancer-provoking factors and the root of the matter. The smoking habit might not be a cause but a mere symptom of a larger pathology. No one yet had definitively isolated the causative factors. There were fine distinctions to be made here. He hoped the reporters would take the pains necessary to grasp his fine shades of meaning and to quote him exactly. There were percentages of risk. More than that, he wouldn't say.

The reporters went over and over the same ground. Was the Director saying that there was no connection between smoking and cancer?

Had the reporters been listening, or only scribbling?

Listening. And trying to understand. Where was the misunderstanding? What *was* the Director trying to say?

It went back and forth like that. Clearly, the reporters could not discern, or would not buy, Dr. Alkavist's fine distinctions.

The Alkahest droned on. He invoked the tentative, open spirit of scientific inquiry.

One reporter asked him if it wasn't true that a leading cigarette manufacturer was contributing something to the expenses of the summer program.

Dr. Alkavist categorically denied this.

Naomi was busy working on her cultures in her lab upstairs when the reporters left. Aunt Ethel came around on a surprise tour of inspection. She was visibly tense and her voice had a sharp edge. She warned Naomi that her lab was a mess, and that it had to be straightened immediately.

There was an ovarian transplant operation scheduled for four that afternoon. Stevie Conroy was first assistant. Stevie was shaky and felt unwell afterwards, although the operation had been a success. Aunt Ethel bundled him off to bed right after the operation, instructing Naomi to absorb Stevie's Rabbit House cleaning assignment next morning, not to fool around with "piddly work" like straightening her lab. Naomi must have looked momentarily baffled; Aunt Ethel assured her that it was all right. She simply wouldn't take any visitors up that way.

"And, oh, yes—this is important. I want you to make sure those two slackers keep at it."

"Two who?"

"You know very well who I mean—Eva and Jerome. Don't pretend you haven't noticed."

Naomi was about to bolt from the room, but was restrained by a firm grip on the shoulder. "Hold your horses —let's get a look at you. You're too pale for my liking. Let me see." Aunt Ethel tugged at the corner of Naomi's eyelid and found it much too white.

"Red meat and spinach, that's what you need. I'll speak to Tertu about it. Have you had a good bowel movement lately?"

Again, right before supper, Aunt Ethel called Naomi into her room. She wanted a rundown on the cleaning of the Rabbit House. She had a glass in her hand and kept swirling the liquid around, the ice cubes clattering. Naomi reported that everything had gone swimmingly. Unfortunately, Aunt Ethel had to disagree with that: the rabbits were still stinking because the crew hadn't gotten far enough under the cages. She asked Naomi most particularly who had done the floor. "Jerome and Eva—am I guessing right? You're not saying anything, so I guess I am."

Naomi said she wasn't sure. Aunt Ethel was sure. Eva and Jerome were altogether too friendly with one another, or rather, Jerome was. In her opinion, he was making an ass of himself over that girl. Eva was a little hussy and not worth anybody's little finger.

"Actually . . ." Naomi refreshed her memory, "it was Alex who did the floor."

"Alex? Well, it doesn't matter who. The whole crew takes the blame. I'm afraid you'll have to go over that floor again."

Aunt Ethel felt she ought to let Naomi know who the

problem children were. "I'm a wise bird. Been around. It's hard to fool me," she said.

Why tell *me?* Naomi wanted to ask. But didn't dare. She listened with increasing unease and distaste, but took care not to miss a single syllable. Isaiah was top of the list, no surprise there. Jerome and Eva were runners-up. Jerome was too superstitious and spent too much time thinking of ways to get to church. Aunt Ethel had found him out—actually caught him down on his knees in the Mouse House early one morning. "There's not much that escapes me," she repeated. As soon as Jerome spotted Aunt Ethel, he'd scrambled to his feet, mumbling something about dropping his pipette and not being able to find all the pieces. "Likely story!" she asserted. "He was on his knees praying like any peasant in the Dark Ages. Can you imagine? In this day and age? He was very red in the face when I caught him in the act—in *flagrante delicto,* as the saying goes. You're too young to know what that means." As for Eva . . . she seemed a nice enough girl at first, but by now she was showing her true colors.

No mention was made of the amount of time Joel and Naomi spent together. Most likely, Aunt Ethel had alerted another informant on that score, keeping everyone on their toes. Naomi held her breath, expecting some sly stab, but it never came. Either Aunt Ethel was not all that wise, or she was storing evidence for future use.

There was somebody crooked in the group, she hinted, because lab coats and socks were disappearing.

"Socks?"

"Yes, socks, I'm unhappy to say it. Socks," she repeated, looking seriously aggrieved. "Any little harassment. It's not a question of need. Somebody in this group is terribly immature."

At this point, Naomi began inching toward the door. But Aunt Ethel wasn't through yet. "Lame brains," she said of the Homays. Here she had given them what any intelligent couple would realize was an ideal situation for the summer. But the Homays were too stupid to see the advantages of it and acted as if they were doing everybody a big favor by coming to the Four Winds. If the facts were known, people would realize that only Frank and herself knew how to run a place like this. They had to keep everyone in tow, including Dr. Alkavist. He was a sweet, sweet man but his head was in the clouds and he rarely touched earth. That press conference was a typical example: a disaster. The Elosons were keeping their fingers crossed but, knowing what newsmen were like, they'd probably come out with some story about collusion with the tobacco companies. It was tough work, keeping everyone in line. The Elosons had taken upon themselves the task of making Dr. Alkavist's dream a living reality. And that was one of the reasons she wanted Naomi to keep her eyes open and to let her in on any trouble brewing. Naomi said nothing to affirm or deny their pact, not one word that might further prolong their conversation. Aunt Ethel went on to say that her only real friends were young people. When you could get youth to say "thank" you and mean it, then you had something. Didn't Naomi agree? Naomi agreed.

By evening, Aunt Ethel was in rare form. Unannounced, she dropped in on Joel and Isaiah. "How did *this* get in here? I suppose it just walked." She pointed to a bedroom scuff under the sink, then discovered a balled-up undershirt on the worktable. Their lab was messy. Messy, but operational—a little worse than usual, but not much. There was an acrid pungency in the air, a trace of ammonia, suggesting an unclean cage. The odor so enraged Aunt Ethel that she ordered Joel and Isaiah to split up. Isaiah was placed in the equipment room, there to be disturbed by anyone using the analytical balance. Aunt Ethel pronounced their project "an unqualified mess." She said she was dividing them up to find out whose fault it was.

The division of animals and equipment took all evening.

Joel and Isaiah had a conference with Dr. Kamin at Spemann Lab the next morning. Joel, who was calmer than Isaiah, recounted the events of the past evening. Kamin stared out the window as he listened; he had an extraordinary length of gaze, and his thoughts seemed very far away.

"And that's how things stand now," Joel concluded. Lamely, he felt, for Kamin's apparent disinterest unnerved him.

"That does it!" said Kamin, coming to life abruptly. "Look at my lab!" His own lab was no paradigm. He was a busy man, he got things done. He knew men with spotless labs who were as sterile as their equipment. Admittedly, he didn't know what Joel and Isaiah's lab had looked like. It was a matter of principle: an outsider had divided up a project going on under his direction without even consulting him. By what right?

Isaiah assured Kamin that Joel and he were working together as before, only going through the motions of separation.

"Who the hell's program director at your place? Never mind, I know. Just let me speak to her."

"Very touchy," Joel cautioned.

"Say I want to check out your equipment. How does that sound?" Kamin seemed determined. He promised to refrain from making comment on anything else at the Four Winds. Would Joel and Isaiah be able to take time out from housework, social period and compulsory baseball to see him when he came? No, on second thought, the sooner he took matters in hand, the better. "Why not today? Will I be able to walk through the front hall?" he asked mischievously.

"Sure," said Isaiah, "as long as you take off your shoes."

They made it back in time for lunch. Kamin took six of the students in his car; there was really only enough room for four or five. Naomi sat on Joel's bony knees. It was as comfortable as perching on doorknobs.

Kamin took pride in his driving, in showing off the hand controls which he'd built for himself. The accelerator and brake were operated by a long lever on the lefthand side of the steering wheel. The device looked like an enlarged stick shift. The students were especially impressed whenever he brought the car to a stop with a flick of the wrist. Kamin smiled, even Isaiah smiled, there was a fine tang in the air, a snap of autumn. Kamin's support gave every one of them a boost. Their condition was known. Things were looking up.

But no one was reckoning on the combined force of Frank and Ethel Eloson.

The three had lunch together, a private session in chambers. Their discussion extended beyond the lunch hour. Members of the dish crew were not allowed in to clear, so they remained standing outside the door, eavesdropping intently—without much success. When they heard chairs scraping within, they readied themselves to cut and run, but then Kamin started up again and Aunt Ethel responded, with voices lowered. It seemed to be a dialogue with only two participants. At one point, they heard Kamin's voice raised and the single word "brilliance!" uttered like an expletive, but nothing else came through as clearly.

When Kamin finally emerged, more than two hours later, he was in a great hurry to get back to the lab. "Waste of time," he pronounced, "who needs it? They want originality, so they say. They don't know how to deal with originality when they do find it. That's their problem, not my problem.

He motioned Isaiah aside. "They've got it in for you," he confided. This came as no news to Isaiah. "Go easy," he urged, "they're wasteful people. They waste themselves most of all."

25

SUNDAY MORNING, Jerome wanted to go to Mass. "Fine," said Aunt Ethel, "that's fine with me. But you'll finish your assigned surgery schedule first." It was an ovarian transplant, a procedure Chief had developed and most of the students had mastered. Yet the operation was a disaster.

Jerome was through well before eleven but, by then, in no mood for church. The students involved huddled together in the hallway afterwards trying to analyze what had gone wrong. Johnny claimed that whenever Chief ligated the fallopian tube he yanked it, and that this was the source of all their troubles. "I've been through the routine twice now. His mind's not on the operation."

"How can you tell?"

"I watch his eyes when I have nothing to do but hold the retractors."

I've never really seen his eyes, thought Naomi.

Herb Smith was passing by and, although uninvited,

couldn't refrain from entering the discussion, insisting that Chief was a fine surgeon who never made a slip. "That man's an artist—not one wasted motion. Every time he makes a stroke of the knife, it does exactly what he wants it to do."

"So he's a virtuoso," Polly agreed. "But if he put less effort into showing off his skill, it would be better all around. Sure, it's impressive when he stands there making his cuts at arm's length. Sure, that's hard to do. But who's it good for?"

"That's right—excuse yourselves and blame him. Take the easy way," Herb answered with some disgust. "I know what I'm talking about, and I'm the only person around here who does."

At lunch, Bob Homay asked to see the captains of the two baseball teams, the second such summons in a matter of weeks. He was still rankling over the last game, when so many asked to be excused and the few who did play scarcely connected with the ball, they were so apathetic. He wanted to see a serious game at the last, a show of group spirit.

As soon as the meal was over, Jerome was called into the private dining room. Aunt Ethel did a lot of shuffling before getting down to business. Jerome studied the portrait of the young woman in the green blouse instead of staring directly at Aunt Ethel. The young woman's eyes eluded him. Chief walked out as Aunt Ethel was warming up to her subject. Did this mean that the summons wasn't all that serious? Or did it mean that the matter was now out of Chief's hands?

Aunt Ethel must have been more nervous than usual,

for she was still leading up to her indictment, making statements that were so broad and sweeping as to give Jerome no purchase. He pricked up his ears at "theory" and "practice"—footholds, and then at the "unity of theory and practice"—a phrase after his own heart. Something about the aims of the summer program.

He thought of an escutcheon for the Four Winds:

THEORY & PRACTICE

And he pictured Theory and Practice as two griffins in mortal combat, or a deathless embrace—not clear which it was. Unless, a mortal embrace?

No, he had it now: a two-headed beast would be just the emblem. Two arms, four legs, chest and cloacal cavity shared equally. One heart, two lungs, one liver, etc. The heads were featureless, but each hand held a radiant eye, as far from the other as possible. . . .

Then he realized that Aunt Ethel had fallen silent, staring at him, waiting for his undivided attention, and that she had a marked strabismus.

The matter was serious; this was his first warning. Jerome's work was not what it should be. He was letting down on his obligations to the group. Was there anything he cared to say on his own behalf?

No.

No?

What he meant to say was that the complaint was too vague.

All right then, to put the matter bluntly: he was seeing too much of Eva, that was a great part of his whole problem. When he asked for more particulars as to what constituted his "whole problem," Aunt Ethel was vague and alluded to Jerome's many outside interests' getting in the way of his work. Only one specific: she described Jerome's part in the last operation as "inexcusable."

That same afternoon there was a lung-transplant operation. Herb failed to preserve the recipient's atrial cuff and, although both rabbits were salvaged, the operation was a fiasco. Aunt Ethel took Herb aside when it was over and asked if he'd been watching every second. "If the assistant is watching properly, there's no possible place for a wrong move. I know."

The Elosons disappeared into their rooms after the operation; they remained sequestered for some hours. Free at last of bells, of scolds, of the fuming and frowning that lay upon the house like some sort of interminable gray weather, Naomi felt her spirit expand. It was as if doors and windows had flown open with a shout. Relief— then outright joy—the feeling was contagious. Jenise scooted through the front hall on a laundry trolley, and Eddy Bartusek revived an ancient ditty:

> Order in the courthouse!
> Chief is eating beans.
> Aunt Ethel's in the bathtub
> Oiling submarines.

Joel and Naomi took advantage of the unscheduled free time to socialize. They sauntered down to the Mouse House hand in hand. No one about. Joel pulled her into a dark corner.

"I want you to feel this," he said.

He was wearing a lab coat over his bathing trunks, and he was wearing nothing else.

"What?"

He took her hand and guided it through the waistband.

Naomi didn't do anything but blink and register the situation: alarming.

She felt his heart beating in his belly.

"What do you plan to do about this?" He began pulling all of her closer. By now, Naomi was definitely interested.

"I—ah—"

Aunt Ethel was at the door. Joel flung Naomi's hand away as if it seared him—

"What's going on here?" Aunt Ethel let the door slam behind her. "Everybody is so jumpy today. And you two—I don't believe it—I didn't see what I saw!"

26

"Squaw winter," Tertu called the first nippy days in August. The early chill promised a snowy winter. And the wasps were building high nests, another sign. Doris had quit in a huff at the end of July. She'd collected what was owing to her and gone off without a word of explanation. Tertu strongly suspected that she'd taken more than was owing. There was a cash box kept in the cupboard which disappeared when the girl left. No one seemed to have noticed, though, and Tertu wasn't about to bring the matter to anyone's attention.

It was too late to hire another girl, with only a little more than three weeks to go. Tertu fussed in the kitchen, banging pots; grease fumed in the pan. She'd gotten used to help with the heavy work and now it was hard for her. The summer had turned out to be more work than the money was worth. Her one cheer was thinking ahead to September, when all the summer folk had packed up and gone. It would be an early fall and a fine one, judging by all the signs. She couldn't be more eager to be on her way.

The day before, she'd found the suggestion box under a big chair with skirts: it had lain there for maybe a month, no one missing it. That said a lot for student housekeeping. It had never been locked. The papers were scattered; she found only two. Half a boxtop from Purina Fox Chow (it must have been a joke), and a slip of yellow paper. She held it at arm's length and read:

The suggestion box ought to
be opened more often.

She replaced the contents and slipped the box back onto the mantelpiece. And that was that: she'd done her part.

The picnic at Breaker's Point on Saturday was to be the big holiday of the summer. Friday night Tertu listened to the radio before turning in. She wanted to make sure of the weather before setting her alarm for three in the morning. "Funny—I mean sunny—and cool tomorrow," the announcer said. Then the tides. Then he asked: "What plans have you made for feeding the birds this winter?"

"Same as last year," she answered, "got my stations set, front porch, back porch, all around the house."

Saturday morning she rose in darkness. The sky slowly lightened, but there was a mist. By the time the sun was up, all the food for the day had been assembled. She decided to mop the kitchen floor herself and spare the students.

It wouldn't take long. Tertu began humming, then recognized the tune and sang the words as they came to her. "Now where are you agoin' to, my pretty maid?" It was a chantey her father had taught her, for pulling up anchor on the outward bound. "Heave away, Ri-o . . ." She couldn't remember the words between or after.

When she'd finished with the floor, she went out to the back porch to greet the early sun. The mist had burned off and the sun was butter on the water. Flat calm. The house seemed to be coasting easy. For a moment, she saw the house after they'd all packed up and gone. That would be it—the shining hour. She saw the Four Winds as a tall proud vessel, setting out to meet the winter seas without skipper or crew. Not long now.

It was so perfectly still. As if there'd never been a storm, never a ripple. This was the time she loved best.

Pack of summer fools, the lot of them, if you wanted her opinion. All that gabbing and proclaiming and declaring, and that la-di-da director of it all, that old man with his head in the sky—his top hamper was surely gone. Always forcing things, when life . . .

Kids too young to know better.

Anna Homay woke before five. The birds were restless; she could hear them clearing their throats, tiny *hems* and *haws*. There was just enough light in the sky to keep her from falling back to sleep.

The window came into focus: ash, opal, fire. Anna

heard a curious sound. It might have been her imagination. Was it? A violin tuning up, first A, then D, a voice softly singing *sol*, then down to *do*, the opening bars of something sweet, Stephen Frosterish, too sweet. Then nothing, the birds again, a water note.

A voice below. Chief's?

"How about those eggs, Tertu?"

"They're coming, slowly . . . so's Christmas."

Bob mumbled in his sleep and turned over away from the light to face the wall. His face was creased in sleep as, no doubt, Anna's was. Pair of old socks, she thought. She let him lie, but his minutes of peace were numbered. The floor was stone-cold. Anna hurried into her clothes.

By quarter to nine they were ready to move. Three cars, three drivers: Bob, Anna and Chief. The Elosons, in their white Mercedes, led the way. Anna took the station wagon with her own children, plus Joel, Isaiah, Naomi, Jenise, and all the edibles. Traffic was light.

Anna caught a glimpse of Jim in the rear-view mirror. He was clutching his talisman, a ridiculous raw potato. It made no sense, but it was the only thing that worked for him against car sickness. They'd tried suggestion, word games, Dramamine, chewing gum. The potato was working so well that Jim had dozed off. His face was askew, his head lolling on his chest and, every now and then, veering to the side, thudding against the window. A thread of spittle gleamed on his chin. He'd probably wake with a headache. Anna didn't look forward to it.

Isaiah, on his own initiative, quietly stuffed a towel between Jim's head and the glass. His thoughtfulness surprised Anna. No one else had noticed, let alone lifted a finger.

Breaker's Point was a well-touristed spit of land only a few miles distant from the Four Winds. The area was provided with a parking lot, tables and barbecue pits on a grassy strip, wire baskets and an outhouse. The picnic area overlooked a seawall, a ledge of broken stones, the sea itself and a small island with a mooring on it but no house in sight.

It was a beautiful day, calm and bright. There must have been an up-wind: the gulls seemed to float.

They unloaded the picnic things on the grass and then, since they had plenty of time before lunch, made their way down to the rocks. Most of the students were content merely to stretch out and bask in the sun on the nearest flat expanse. Bob took his children and a few energetic students around the point to hunt for tidal pools. "Be caref—!" Anna warned. But they were quickly out of earshot.

Anna wandered freely, heading in the direction of the cove.

The cove was a gentle beach, narrow and self-enclosed. The sea lapped quietly here, and the rocks had a different character: they were egg-shaped. Water, working patiently without pause, had softened all edges. In a million years it would be nothing but sand. Anna thought of that time to come without sadness; she was alive in the moment and it didn't seem to matter.

But not alone, it came with a shock to discover she was not alone. Someone was here before her. He was a few yards off. The air was so dazzling she couldn't tell whether he was standing with his back or face to her. As she drew near, he waved.

"Having a good time?" It was Isaiah.

"Yes," she said, inhaling deeply. "I sure am. Aren't you?"

"I don't know," he mumbled.

"That's a funny answer. How can you not know?"

"I saw something back there. Did you see him—the kid with the magnifying glass?"

"The one that was following an ant, trying to study it?"

"He wasn't studying. He was concentrating a beam of sunlight on it. He was trying to incinerate it," Isaiah said portentously, "didn't you realize?"

Yes, that's just the sort of thing Isaiah *would* notice, Anna thought. He looks for it, he picks it out and, maybe, he even calls it forth. He's trying to spoil my day, my one day. I'm not going to let it happen.

"How do you know what he was trying to do? You don't know!" she answered.

He flinched at her tone, but said nothing.

She turned and walked on, bristling with irritation, determined to enjoy this day of freedom, her one day of real vacation. With his fiddle he's a nice boy, she thought. But without it he's nothing but an enormous case of hives. She continued walking, more slowly now.

Hadn't she been unfair? Maybe. They'd both seen the same thing: a boy following the meanderings of a tiny ant with a large magnifying glass. The rest was anyone's guess. Neither Anna nor Isaiah could be sure.

As soon as she rounded the bend, Anna regretted her harshness. She turned back to say something mollifying, but failed to find Isaiah at the cove. She'd spoken her mind—all right, was that such a crime? There was nothing to feel sorry about, she kept telling herself, but her eyes ached from squinting and somehow the day was already dimmed.

Isaiah was nowhere near the cove.

27

Bob was up at the farthest jut of land. Anna signaled him to come to her. He misunderstood, waved assurance, shouted back that it was perfectly safe—firm ground—but when she stood and persisted in waiting, he left the group he was with and returned to the broad beach to join her.

"What's up? We were having a big time."

Anna explained.

Bob saw no cause for alarm: "You think he's lost? What makes you think that?"

"I just know," she said lamely. "Where could he go?"

"*How* do you know?"

"I feel certain. I'm sure of it." Something told her. A hunch? A pang?

"Irrelevant! It's irrelevant how you feel. You've got no facts and it isn't a reasonable assumption," said Bob, speaking for reason. "Chances are he's out of sight—off sulking someplace. I'll check the outhouse first."

Isaiah wasn't in the outhouse—the fact that he wasn't seemed to upset Bob excessively. "That son of a gun!" he pronounced.

"You've only checked out the first possibility," Anna reminded him.

"Thinks he can do anything he damn pleases, does he? He'll have to be brought in tow. Even *my* patience is worn thin, Anna, and everyone knows I'm a patient man."

Walking stiffly with the effort to look casual, the Homays canvassed the beach. The Elosons were sitting up on the slope, under the shade of some trees. Chief was reading a book. Aunt Ethel and Tertu were busy shelling peas. Aunt Ethel waved. Anna was too preoccupied to notice; Bob waved back.

"It's been a rough summer for me, for the children especially. I hope you realize."

"You think it's been fun for me, Anna? Think it's been easy? That it's my fault?"

"No, not your fault, never anybody's fault. Everybody's fault." Words—what was the use? Everyone was trapped.

There was no sign of Isaiah.

Bob went up ahead to organize a search party of students. Anna returned more slowly. She picked her way carefully. Her vision was sharpened now. She saw a battered scow she hadn't noticed before; it was only accidentally moored, its painter snagged in the rubble of the beach. Abandoned or lost? she wondered. Oarless, it looked as if it had made its way alone to the shore.

She noticed the debris: rings from beer cans, a fractured winch, a comb, an empty packet of corn plasters, a swizzle stick, bits of bottle glass, soft-sided and milky from the stroking of the sea. Anna saw now as she had not seen before, with a painful distinctness, each rock unique and absolute, unlike any other.

One by one, the search party set out, fanning in all directions. Within half an hour they had established that Isaiah was nowhere about.

"Where you been? Circling round and round like that," Aunt Ethel began as soon as Anna rounded the bend again.

"Beachcombing."

"We do things here in a group. I'm surprised at you, Anna. Everybody together. I'd appreciate a hand at serving here."

"Just a sec. Got to have a word with Bob—be right with you."

"What next?" Anna and Bob were stumped. There was nothing left for them to do but to organize a larger search party and get to work on the roads. What was Isaiah wearing? A dark sweatshirt—Anna thought it was green. Bob could have sworn it was blue, navy blue. Pants—chinos or jeans? Anna couldn't remember. How could she *not* remember? Were they light or dark? Dark, she thought, but she'd been looking into the sun. He could look like any other boy or blend with the foliage, for he was wearing nothing distinguishable. Aunt Ethel would have to be told.

"You do it, Bob. I can't."

"Anna, you're a shrinking violet. That's your whole trouble."

As it turned out, no one had to tell Aunt Ethel. The students were beginning to cluster around the lunch tables when it occurred to her that she hadn't seen Isaiah in an hour or more.

"Has anyone seen that boy?" she called out.

The Homays explained. Aunt Ethel listened without comment, then insisted on joining the hunt. Anna thought that wouldn't be necessary.

"He's my responsibility, Anna—I have to go. Lunch can wait."

Half of the students stayed back to cover the shorefront with Chief and Tertu; they kept the station wagon. Bob Homay and Herb Smith set out on foot. Aunt Ethel took the Mercedes alone, and Anna filled the Homay car with students.

Slowly, they backed out; slowly, hugging the shoulder, they joined the main road. There were many detours along the way and they took every one.

It was midafternoon by the time they reached the gate of the Four Winds. They had not stopped for lunch and everyone was out of temper. "I could eat a horse," Stevie said glumly. "It isn't fair for one person to screw things up for everybody else."

"Aunt Ethel will skin him, she'll fry him," predicted Tom Li. "She'll eat him alive," he added with a certain zest.

The drivers stepped out of their cars to confer. "I saw a porcupine making for the deep woods, but that's all I saw," Anna reported. "His needles lay flat. He was so slow, it's no wonder they need protection."

"Don't play games, Anna. It's about time we faced

facts. I'm going up to the house and I'm going to call the police. He'll pay for this." Decisive words, in a voice thin and tremulous.

With Anna's car in the lead, they passed the gate. As they neared the house, Anna heard something strange.

She turned off the motor, held her breath, and listened. The air swelled with sound.

The sound of a fiddle.

Aunt Ethel, in her silent Mercedes, must have heard it before anyone else.

Anna jerked on the hand brake and rushed from the car. She wanted to be the first to reach him, she had to get there before—

But Aunt Ethel was close on Anna's heels, and the students swarmed after the two women. They gathered at the open door and stood there, silent, on the threshold.

He was standing with his back to the door, playing to a gallery of stairs. It was something so dark, brooding and sonorous that Anna could have sworn it was a cello she heard.

"Of all the gall!" Aunt Ethel was the first to break the spell.

He continued the andante.

"Listen when I talk to you, boy!"

Continuing. Same even pace.

"This is it, Isaiah. The absolute final warning—get that? I don't care if you're one day short of finishing up the summer. You hear me? This is *it*. You'll be packing your bags so fast—you hear?"

He heard. He let his bowing arm fall, ending on a sour note. For a moment he did not move, but stood there stiffly, fiddle tucked under his arm, as if for an ovation. He made a point of avoiding Anna's eyes.

"And now you'll listen to what I have to say. This is absolutely your last chance. One slightest infraction of the rules from here on out and you've had it. I'm talking about discipline. I'm talking about group spirit. About selfishness—"

Isaiah stood there, nodding once to each accusation. When the harangue was over, he carefully loosened his bow, cradled the instrument in its case, and locked it. There was a tiny clicking sound of satisfaction made by the lock as it snapped shut. "That done!" it seemed to say. For an instant Anna thought Aunt Ethel had made the sound.

Naomi stood to the right of Anna and a little behind. Only Aunt Ethel had spoken. It was a strange scene.

There was a scattering of onlookers at the door, then a mob; they seemed to coalesce in relation to Isaiah's separateness. Gapers and smilers, all.

With his fiddle in action, he had the power of flight. Once he let his bowing arm fall, he surrendered to alien powers and was a caged, a cornered thing.

He'd been inconsiderate of everyone but himself, Naomi granted that much. But she was not prepared to call it "sub-standard behavior," as Herb pronounced afterwards and repeated to everyone who'd listen, feeling he'd coined a wonderfully clever expression. What was "standard behavior?" The phrase made her shudder.

Standing there at the door, Naomi was conscious of

body warmth on all sides of her, the warmth of the pack. As Isaiah's force ebbed, theirs waxed strong. It was a strange equation. Something troubling in it, very troubling, something that needed serious thinking over. If only she could find a moment in which to think.

The days that followed were lost in scurrying.

28

THAT SUNDAY EVENING, as every other Sunday evening, Dr. Alkavist showed up for his usual sermon. Anna wasn't sure she understood any of it, but it seemed to her that he began by calling a spade a spade. He was going to talk about aging and had nothing particularly good to say about it. He quoted the great master of geriatrics, a man called Alex Comfort: "Senescence has no function—it is the subversion of function." He said this twice.

Anna studied Dr. Alkavist's face as he spoke, saw how it was slipping down, coming unstuck, and knew her own face was only temporary, biding its time, resting loosely on the bones. His gesturing hands were cumbered, caught in their heavy fretwork of veins.

"Let's not sentimentalize," said Dr. Alkavist, spreading his knobbed fingers. "Senescence is an evil, but is it a necessary evil? An inherent or fundamental feature of life? I wonder. No one has conclusively proven it to be."

He paused for a sip of water, waiting for his opening to sink in. If this was revolutionary matter, no one seemed to appreciate it. The students slumped in their chairs, expressionless.

"No proof," he went on. "Senescence is nothing more than a name for the many changes that accompany increasing age, changes which are associated circumstantially, not causally, with decreasing expectation of life. A set of correlations in need of explanation—that's all we have.

"Since senescence is not an inevitable process, the attempt to find one fundamental cellular property to explain all instances of such change is very likely misplaced. Cells, even adult human cells, can be kept alive indefinitely by means of cell culture in vitro." He mentioned trees, cultures of chick cells, plaice and sponge. "Certain forms of life, especially among the fish family, never age. Certain forms of life never die."

All Anna could think of was the amoeba. She wondered how it felt going on forever. It occurred to her that the primeval amoeba was alive and well in the world at that very moment, existing in trillionfold and more, multiplied endlessly in unwearying sameness. But she was losing the drift of the talk. Dr. Alkavist was on to something new.

Not really new. "So many of the basic theories accounting for the aging process rest, at bottom," he insisted, "on folklore or a biblical sense of sin. The most obvious of these is the belief that senescence and death are the price to be paid for sexuality. Why does a price have to be paid for sexuality? *That* has to be explained. . . ." He left it to them whether a theory based on guilt and a sense of primeval debt could have any credence as science.

Aside from biblical notions, there were the common-sense theories, based on commonsense limitations of thought. There were the wear-and-tear theories and the fixed-total-energy theories, all of which relied on easy analogies to machines. But living organisms were not mechanisms precisely in this respect: living organisms were self-regulating and self-regenerating.

There were the growth-inhibition theories, but these led to their own contradictions. "If you want my personal opinion, and it's no more than that—an opinion—the only theories worthy of consideration on biological grounds are the metabolic theories. These are based on a well-established inverse relationship between length of life and rate of living. Factors which retard development or reduce metabolism tend to postpone senescence in many organisms. The heavy buildup of collagen in connective tissues is clearly associated with the loss of flexibility in aging."

Ah, collagen . . . Anna recognized the word. She'd read it somewhere, some magazine. Isn't that what happens in the healing of wounds—collagen buildup? Anna wondered. So aging would mean that the entire body takes on the texture of a healing wound? She doubted very much whether Dr. Alkavist meant to say anything of the kind, but she had to keep her mind going somehow, anyhow, to stay awake.

"What we should work on is the slowing up of metabolism. Controlled retardation is not the same thing as reversal, but a step in that direction. Reversal of the aging process is not yet in man's power, but its day will come. Its day will someday come. I offer a toast to the quest—to the obsolescence of senescence!" (Anna couldn't help hearing a rhyme.) He raised his glass of chalky water and drank to that. It was a toast he offered with some envy, he told his listeners. For, surely, he would not be there to see the day.

Again, he reminded them that this was no pipe dream. They had only to think of the continuing division of the cells of a chick's heart in culture, long after the donor's life span had passed. True, there were cellular changes in that time, but this only posed a problem for further study. There was more to be known, always more to be known. He urged the young students gathered before him now— the young who would someday know what it was to be old—to dedicate themselves to the substance of his toast. It was from deeply rooted humanistic convictions that he spoke.

"All religions have fostered the notion of human finitude—and well they might. All religions have traded on the fear of death for their domination over the minds of men. I stand opposed to all pieties of fear—are you with me? I stand at the crossroads of the future—are you there?"

He stood like Tinker Bell on an empty stage, clamoring for their support, waiting.

Many heads were bowed, faces folded down. Aunt Ethel began the applause; it flickered, caught, soon the room was full of hands beating the air. Anna found herself clapping as hard as anyone. She pounded for the old man standing there in his rags of skin, and for dreams. She pounded to shout down the dark. And then, abruptly, she let her hands drop. What were they doing? They were beating back the specter of death as furiously as any tribesmen with drums.

There was more when the clapping ceased, a hundred learned periphrases. Anna sensed the intricacy of the fabric which Dr. Alkavist was weaving, but could only follow a single thread and, even that, imperfectly. Whatever associations she had with words and phrases were accidental and irrelevant, of this she was certain. She had no head at all for abstractions. The simplest abstract progression fazed her and fizzled in the end: one, two . . . plenty. She'd never been much of a student; it hadn't ever bothered her that she wasn't. Even when she took her exams, she'd dotted her *i*'s with flower faces and hearts, wasting so much essential time. It was a wonder that she ever passed.

For the students at the Four Winds it was different. The classroom was the arena in which these children most intensely lived, achieved their greatest victories, savored their deepest loves and joys, and suffered their most crushing defeats. While life had always been on the other side of the classroom window for Anna. For her the classroom was nothing but an anteroom, a place of fidgets and long parentheses, waiting for the real thing—whatever *that* would be. And she was still waiting, wasn't she? She'd been an idler and a dreamer all her days and, chances were, always would be.

Dr. Alkavist dreamed, too, but with a certain discipline. After a while, Anna was only able to take in the colors of the words: progeria, hydranth, ischemia, lesion, clones, metazoan. The mayfly lives but a day, yet in that day . . . No, she made that up.

Age chimeras, euplasia, foamy cytoplasm, extrusions, weeping of serum, lumen . . . The students were excused immediately after the lecture; they would have to buckle down. Final reports were soon due. The Elosons, assisted by Bob and Anna Homay, gathered in the wooden folding chairs. The chairs creaked and groaned, rackety with irreversible age.

29

"HAVE YOU NOTICED?" Joel and Naomi were setting up for breakfast.

"Noticed what?"

"Hey, pass me a couple of butter knives, will you?"

"Noticed *what*, Joel?"

"Isaiah is acting strange lately."

"So what else is new?"

"No, I mean stranger than usual."

"Like how?"

"Nothing I can put my finger on exactly. Just little things."

"Like what?"

"Well, yesterday was his birthday. He got two cards in the mail. He looked at the envelopes for a long time, he kept studying them. I asked him: 'Why don't you open them?' But he didn't answer, he acted like he didn't hear."

"Not opening them—that's not so strange," Naomi

replied. "Me—I wouldn't wait. I couldn't. But that's just me. Different people are different."

"But he acted like he didn't hear. He does it all the time now. He hangs up on me. The line goes dead. And, the point is, he still hasn't opened those cards."

"Okay, it's a little odd. Anything else?"

"He sits up all night. He doesn't sleep."

"How do you know? You sleep, don't you?"

"I can't tell for sure, but I know one thing. I'm sleeping less and less as I see more of it. It's spooky, it gives me an eerie feeling. Him—just sitting there on the edge of the bed, his feet on the cold floor so he's sure not to fall asleep. Just sitting there and staring at nothing."

"Why don't you tell him to lie down and go back to sleep?"

"I do. But he doesn't answer. He stares. His eyes look so—empty. See if you don't notice."

"Maybe it's that experiment you're doing. It's ear-blasting. Even from a distance that sound makes my teeth ache, all my fillings. If he's at all sensitive to harsh sound —and I'm sure he must be—it must drive him out of his head."

"You don't think maybe *I'm* sensitive? You don't think I'm capable of suffering?"

"Know what I really think? I think the pressure's getting to you, Joel. The cracks are beginning to show."

"And I think he's going to murder us all."

Naomi began to laugh and Joel did too, though grudgingly, in spite of himself. He was really worried, Naomi saw that now. She made up her mind to watch Isaiah more carefully.

The opportunity presented itself almost at once. Cleaning their labs that morning, Naomi and Isaiah shared a broom and dustpan. Naomi had the broom first. They set to work.

"Do you hear a bell ringing?" Isaiah asked.

"No—not now."

"Not even faintly?"

"Bells in this house never ring faintly."

"That's funny. I keep hearing this ringing, this humming in my ear. All the time, just this little tiny hum . . . you know, like a mosquito. I can't get it out and I can't really hear anything else."

"Guess you miss your fiddle. Cheer up, you'll get back to it. Summer's nearly over." Naomi took a good long look at Isaiah. There *was* something wrong. He seemed thin as a rail, but that wasn't it, he'd always been lean. His cheeks had shadows in them and, though with his glasses it wasn't easy to be sure, there seemed to be dark, wasting shadows around his eyes, fever shadows.

Starting the second week of August, the crunch was on. Steady pressure. To Naomi, it looked as if she'd never be able to finish. By Thursday there was an air of general panic prevailing—only two weeks to go! All the students, without exception, agreed that it was unfair to bring in guest lecturers at this point. They hadn't the time or patience to concentrate on anything beyond their immediate projects. It came as a gift to no one to learn that the eminent Dr. Bellev was gracing them with a lecture on precursor blood cells in the embryonic mouse. Any other time, fine and welcome, but not now.

Now the students arrived as close to starting time as

possible. They were hoarding minutes and seconds, and when they spoke, it was of nothing but typing schedules and deadlines. Bellev's fine talk was wasted on them.

Unforgivable again when just the next day they were called down for another meeting, this one unscheduled and without any pretension to content.

It had been stormy and gray out all day; the seminar room was glaring in contrast. A fluorescent light winked on and off, on its way to fade-out but too early to change. The room was small, used only for technical conferences and study groups. It was very bare, except for a blackboard on an easel, two rows of tables with plastic tops—faked to look like wood—and a great number of metal chairs.

As far as Naomi could tell, no one but Chief and Aunt Ethel knew why the meeting had been called. They sat up at the front of the room, saying nothing and smoking intently. They must have been sitting there for some time, because there was a litter of butts in front of them. They kept lighting new cigarettes in unison.

The Homays sat side by side without touching or looking at one another. Naomi wondered whether they'd been interrupted in the middle of a quarrel; it certainly looked that way. Once Bob Homay brushed his wife's elbow and she jumped a little—not much, but enough to be noticeable.

Aunt Ethel called the meeting to order by coughing: one—two—at first deliberately, and then explosively. Spot on the glottis, maybe. She coughed and coughed, trying to shake it off.

They waited for Chief to fill in, but he failed to take up the initiative and continued to smoke in silence.

216

Finally Aunt Ethel regained her composure and began: "I guess everybody knows why we're here."

Silence.

"Well then, let me make it crystal clear. I'm not going to beat around the bush. We've come up against some discipline problems this year, problems we never expected in a group handpicked as this one."

"Excuse me, Mrs. Eloson, but is everybody here? Aren't some—isn't someone missing? Should I ring the bell again?" Anna Homay asked.

"Missing?" Aunt Ethel looked up with some surprise. "Someone not responding to three bells," she said coolly, "then it can't be helped. Three signals were enough for everyone else. Who's the privileged character around here? The rest of you—anyone who feels like it—can pass on the discussion."

"But I believe—" Anna didn't bother to finish the sentence. It was perfectly evident who was missing.

Aunt Ethel pursed her lips. She held the butt end of her cigarette between two stained fingers; she studied it with great care. The thing was smoked down as far as could be. One last time. She applied it to her lips: a gray button with a ring of fire. One bitter breath. She quashed the butt, then took up the story from the point of interruption.

Money was missing from the collection the students had taken up for Dr. Alkavist's end-of-summer gift.

They shifted glances, all of them.

Anna asked where the kitty had been kept.

"In the kitchen cupboard."

Bob Homay bit his lip. Naomi wondered what *that*

meant. As if anyone suspected him of being the guilty one!

"Then anyone working in the kitchen could have easily walked off with it, am I right?" Anna Homay continued.

"It's an inside job, Anna, if that's what you're getting at. The question is—who would have wanted to do it? It's not that much money, it's more a gesture of the kind that's become so tiresomely familiar this summer. Only someone opposed to our program would have done it. Somebody terribly immature. These are the facts we must bear in mind." Aunt Ethel leaned back with the air of a lawyer resting a case.

"Facts? What are the facts?" Anna's voice went shrill. "And you call yourselves scientists—you make me laugh! You haven't a leg to stand on. Why not blame Tertu? Why not Alfred? Why not Doris? Why *not* Doris? Now there's an idea. She left—suddenly!" Her voice, her hands, were shaking with the enormity of her unprecedented rise to assertion.

Anna's face was flaming with passion. There was a hush. Everyone stared at her.

"Jesus, what was that about?" Leo whispered. "What's the provocation?"

No explanation was forthcoming. Anna shoved her chair into the table by way of final punctuation, then turned her back on the group and made for the door.

"Why do you always stick up for him, Anna? What's he ever done for you?" Aunt Ethel's voice was little more than a whisper. Anna was already gone.

Bob Homay glared at the surface of the table, traced a stenciled woodprint with his thumb. Then he too stood up and said quietly: "I'm afraid I can't be party to this either. Really, I wouldn't name names if I were you." He seemed to be addressing Chief.

Chief coughed once, decorously.

Eyes on his feet, Bob Homay advanced to the door.

Aunt Ethel watched him go. Her eyes had a fuzzy, unfocused look that suggested migraine. The silence continued longer than it should have.

For most of the students it was a silence of deep or apparent mystification. But not for Naomi. She knew perfectly well where the discussion had been leading, she'd been aware for quite a while. It was not an accredited way of knowing; she didn't know how she knew; all the same, she knew. And yet she stayed on, they all did. They all sat there. In silence. We're all . . . battery mice, she thought.

Aunt Ethel's voice was small when she spoke again. Clearly, her heart had gone out of the discussion. "Who's mentioned names? Nobody," she said. "It could be anyone, anyone at all, kitchen staff included—though, I'm sure, not Tertu. So I'm not accusing anyone. But we ought to be alert to these things happening. And we're all going to have to make good the loss. That means a dollar more from each of you. It's unfair, I know, that the innocent should pay the price, but that's how it is."

How it is. They went on to discuss work crews, shirkers and laggers and, although Isaiah's name was not mentioned, he was denoted quite plainly by repeated references to "people with so many other interests they can't remember what their assignments are."

Jenise slipped off her watch and placed it on the table

in front of her. Every few minutes she'd lift it up and take a close look at it, then fidget with the stem and set it down again, shaking her head with disbelief.

Chief studied the migrations of smoke.

At last, to end on a positive note, Aunt Ethel proposed that a committee of three be set up to send invitations for the certificate-granting ceremony at the end of the summer. She kept referring to it as "graduation." There were no volunteers and no nominations. Only an enemy would have wished an extra task on anyone else at that point, time was so precious. Aunt Ethel had no choice but to appoint a committee. She named Hans, Naomi and Herb.

30

NAOMI HAD two Basics pending. She'd saved her skeletal preparations of mice for the last; they were simple enough if you had your wits about you. She had no problem with the Spalteholtz technique. The specimen came out intact, beautifully preserved in glycerine, the bones an almost translucent claret. But she ran into trouble with the Grüneberg technique. She left the skeleton out to dry on a piece of filter paper. Too rushed to wait with it, she turned to another project. Since the bones were separate, they took flight with the first breeze. Joel and Naomi spent more time than they could afford on their hands and knees, sweeping the floor with their fingers. There were cracks between the boards and where the baseboard met the wall. They retrieved the long bones, all the ribs, skull and pelvis, but the delicate vertebrae were irretrievably scattered.

"Would you two get out from under foot?" Polly

found it difficult to move. They rose stiffly. No help for it—Naomi had to begin her Grüneberg over again from scratch.

There was no letup at all that week. The Alkahest showed up for his usual Sunday evening inspirational in the common room, as though this were a week like any other.

He had a dream of beginnings: of one hundred high-school students living out the summer in tents, doing basic research, "living science, really living it." He wanted to see a formal school established under the aegis of Spemann Lab. The students would live in tents, he repeated. This was important. The amenities wouldn't matter. There was something to be said for tents, Naomi decided, it would take care of housework, anyway.

Graduating from this school, the students would go forth as missionaries. No, this wasn't simply a dream. The Alkahest planned to present a definite proposal, down to the last dollar and cent required, at the annual meeting of the trustees in September.

After he finished speaking, the students were told to remain in their seats for a little discussion. "I'd like some feedback from you," he urged.

This was a new note. The Elosons usually announced their intentions, no consultation required, and the students simply complied. But the Alkahest seemed to want their consent. He wanted the students to like his plan.

It was puzzling. One or, at most, two of the students would be returning for a second summer, so their approval hardly mattered.

The Alkahest settled heavily into one of the chairs in

the front row. Naomi noticed that the Homays were not present.

Chief was the first to speak up. He rose to his feet and turned around to face the students. Accept or reject Dr. Alkavist's plan, it's entirely up to you, he said.

This made even less sense. Something, clearly, was expected of the students. With time at a premium, they were anxious to know what it was, to comply, and to have done with it as speedily as possible.

He went on. The students could do more than accept Dr. Alkavist's plan; they could present it as their own proposal. In fact, it would look that much stronger if it were sent forth from this grateful student group as a legacy for those who would follow. Chief's words were in behalf of endorsement, but he delivered them in such a monotone that they came out with exactly the opposite effect. "As I said, it's up to you," he concluded, leaving the students more bewildered than before.

Aunt Ethel was more passionate. She took the lectern next and made quite a speech. The students would have to be mature to be able to accept Dr. Alkavist's challenge. Afterwards, Naomi was never quite sure of the exact phrasing, but she did remember the word "mature," used several times, each time heavily underscored. And "brilliant idea"—Aunt Ethel dwelled on its brilliance at length. Still, Naomi hadn't the foggiest notion of what was expected from the students at this point. What were they supposed to be mature enough to do?

The answer was rapidly forthcoming.

Aunt Ethel moved that a resolution be composed and sent to the Board of Trustees that very evening.

No harm in that, everyone seemed to agree.

But they quibbled at great length over the wording of the resolution. Whereas . . . whereas . . . Be it resolved that . . . Naomi found herself nodding, dropping off with unprecedented weariness. She was bored to death and exhausted. Her left foot was asleep and, since she couldn't get up and stamp, she began rubbing the sole against the chair leg in front of her. Wood to wood, she thought idly. Where had she heard that before?

She'd missed the text of the resolution. Something about "encouraging more devoted students of the sciences."

Stevie Conroy rose to his feet to say that this sounded like a slur on the present crop of students. How could any students be more devoted than this group?

Chief assured Stevie that he'd misunderstood. Aunt Ethel read the text of the resolution once more, placing the stresses carefully. The point, she explained, was not to encourage students who were more intensely devoted than the present group. No one questioned the intensity of this group. The point was to encourage more, that was to say, greater numbers of such devoted students as those gathered here.

Stevie fell back into his seat, smiling with relief, appeased. More in this vein of delicate analysis followed until Eddy Bartusek moved that all further nit-picking cease, a move greeted by a chorus of seconds.

Finally they voted on the resolution: overwhelmingly affirmative with one abstention—who? Isaiah. How typical. No one asked for his reasons, and he voiced none. What was a resolution? Only words. How could it hurt?

What would it have cost Isaiah to vote yes? Nothing. It would have given an extra puff to an old man's pipe dream. Let the trustees vote it down. Some people went out of their way to be difficult, just to be different.

Isaiah sat in the back of the room, in the next to last row. He was so far back that he was surrounded on all sides by a ring of empty chairs. Naomi wondered why he took all that trouble to further isolate himself. He was isolated enough as it was.

When the students got up to leave, he signaled Naomi aside.

"I'd like to talk to you," he said.

"Who, me?"

"Who else?"

"What's up, Isaiah?"

"Hold on. Let the others go."

The rest of the students filtered out. Naomi fanned through the pages of her loose-leaf impatiently. When the room cleared, she reminded him of their deadlines. "I don't have much time to spare, I don't know about you."

"Me? I got all the time in the world," he said tonelessly. "It's all over with me." He stared at her without expression of any kind. It must have been his acne. He had medicinal paste plastered over his forehead and cheeks. It had stiffened the skin like a mask. "I'll only take a minute of your time," he added with some formality. "I need money, that's the long and short of it. All I've got is two dollars. I don't want to ask Kamin."

"Okay, but why me? I mean, I can spare you a few dollars but I'm no Rockefeller or anything."

"You're from home, that makes you almost family. I

don't mean the money should come from you. If you'd ask the others, they'd help. If *you* asked."

"What for? At this stage of the game—when do you think you'll have time to spend it? I don't get it. You're supposed to be buckling down. It's only two weeks to finish now—less than two really, because the last two days don't count."

"I'm going home now."

"Aw, come off it! You stuck it out so far—don't be a baby."

"Not my choice. I've been kicked out."

"It's a threat, you know that. You've been through it before."

"No—this is it, this time it's for real. Joel's supposed to take over my projects. He doesn't know yet. They'll tell him tonight."

"That's too crummy to be true. Why not wait and see?"

"All I'm asking for is a couple of bucks. I'll hitch a ride to Boston. Then I'll hole up with my friend Morty in Cambridge for a while. I lied to Chief. Told him I called my father, but I only called Boston. I can't go home like this. You don't know what it's like. I've got two sisters counting on me, and my old man believes in responsibility, up with the bootstraps, willpower, the whole bit. Know what he thinks of music? He's got a tin ear and all he can think of is this old man who stands outside Carnegie Hall, grinding his bow to dust—for pennies! He wears these picturesque clothes—you know, a filthy raincoat that must have belonged to a larger man, sneakers. He's always there; even when it's snowing, he stands under the canopy and plays with woolen gloves—it makes very little difference in the fingering. He's that bad. When somebody who looks French passes by, he starts up the Marseillaise. Otherwise, it's always the same. A little souped-up Massenet, a humoresque—Dvořák, Brahms' Hungarian dances done with a lot of brio, and some very romantic Schumann—it comes out sadder than hell. It's all done with a lot of feeling. Too much. People pay in hope of shutting him up. . . . You're looking at me funny and you're not saying anything."

"I think I've seen him. What can I say?"

"If you've seen him, you know how he sounds. When people come out of the concert, he's there, worse than all the street noises. They want to hold on to the concert, what they remember of the real music, so they pay him to go away. But he never goes. First time Pop saw him, he turned to me in a flash and said: 'That what you want to be? You want to end up like *that?*' And maybe I would end up like that—who knows what he wanted to be? Or how he hears himself? I can't get him out of my mind. My old man may be tone-deaf, but what if he's right? Pop works hard. I see it, I'm not blind, it's not work he wants to do. He's trapped. That's what responsibility means—trapped whichever way you turn. It eats him up that he never finished high school. 'Education is everything,' he says. He's an assistant druggist and he'll never be anything else—the guy who counts the pills and works the cash register, the one without the pharmacy degree. He always wanted to be a doctor. And I'm supposed to make up for it, see? So how can I go home now? Just do me a favor and ask some of the kids for me. Whatever they can spare. I'll pay it back soon as I can. I'm clearing out before the first bell tomorrow, it's the only way. No waiting around for Aunt Ethel to make arrangements—why should I give her the satisfaction? I need the money now."

"I'm willing to make you a bet—it's a threat. Anyone would think you were asking for it, you know. You haven't made it easy, but if they've kept you on this far, they'll keep you on a few days more, that's only reasonable. *People are reasonable*. How much you want to bet?"

"I know it's not a threat."

"I can't believe it. And how do you think you'd get out of your family knowing? Chief would call your father himself if he meant business. First let's find out what's what. Make sure. I don't know *anything*."

"You *want* not to know. Let me tell you something—"

"Look, Isaiah, right now I've got no time."

"I get the message," he said.

"Some other time." Naomi stood at the door. She stared at her suspended left foot for an instant, then, unsteadily, put her weight upon it. She almost tripped—she'd been sitting too long—then went forward. She walked out the door, it took willpower. She could feel Isaiah standing there, just beyond the threshold. She could feel his eyes on her back.

Too much high drama; she refused to have any part of it. Isaiah was wrong. He'd see.

In a tearing hurry, she returned to her lab. She skimmed through her notebooks and read the same sentences over and over, each time with diminishing returns.

The better part of her mind continued the conversation with Isaiah, an endless conversation with no foreseeable conclusion. How he battered at her! Forcing her to choose when there was so much wrong on either side—

She began her report on the Grüneberg technique.

Object:
Materials:
Method:

The description should have been mechanical, but nothing came. Having "saved time," Naomi could not use it. Faithful to her decision, to her error—if it was an error—she could not return to Isaiah and hear him out. If he read this as betrayal, it couldn't be helped. She suspected everything was over between them. Yet when had there ever been anything between them?

"We aren't related," she'd written home, meaning not in the literal sense of cousins. But, of course, they were related. He threatened her; she refused him from the first. He cast doubt on everything she prided herself on being: independent, objective, balanced, clear. "You want not to know. . . ." How his words rankled. Unfair. Untrue. She was passionate to know—everything!

He was a spoiler, creating disruption, doubt, dissension wherever he went. A wild cell in an orderly tissue. Pitting himself against everyone from the start, he never belonged to this group; he might never belong to any group. How could he? He knew nothing of compromise, admitted no middle ground.

He'd met his match in Aunt Ethel. But he was the

stronger of the two, anyone could see that. With his overwhelming sense of self, his pride of purpose, he had the firmest of standing grounds. She was shaky, desperate, fragile.

Then why had *he* sounded so shaky this evening?

When they gathered in the kitchen for the evening snack, Isaiah was nowhere in sight. Joel was late in coming down; he arrived with the news that he was taking over Isaiah's projects, effective immediately. He didn't know if he could handle the extra work, but Isaiah was close to finishing up, so he supposed he could. It would be worth a try.

"You should refuse," Naomi said at once. "Whether you could finish up the work or not. It's a kind of theft."

"Believe me, I argued. They told me I had no choice. Either I finished up his projects or they'd go unfinished, that's all the choice I got. Go and talk to Chief yourself. Or, better yet, try Aunt Ethel. All I can think of now is to get hold of the Alkahest. Since it's late, we can't do that before morning."

Isaiah had turned over the rough drafts of his reports and given Chief a quick rundown on animals and equipment. Joel thought Isaiah was taking it all with extraordinary calm. It was most unlike him. At the moment, he was in the bedroom packing up. He didn't want any visitors, he'd made that perfectly plain. Anyone who felt he had to say goodbye could do so in the morning. "Frankly, I think it would be a farce," was what he'd said.

Aunt Ethel made the formal announcement of dismissal over molasses doughnuts and apple cider. They were taking this action reluctantly, she explained. This was the first time and, she hoped, the last time—ever. They were doing it to teach Isaiah a lesson before it was too late, it was for Isaiah's own good. "Isaiah didn't measure up. And, honestly, I don't think he even tried to measure up."

Chief stood just behind Aunt Ethel as she spoke, yet remained silent, curiously distant.

31

Eva is interested in Alex and it's really no news to anyone, least of all to me. He's captain of the Basenjis and Eva is his outfielder. She's not very good, but he's very forgiving and they usually win in spite of her. No wonder, considering the opposing team—my team, the Buttercups. Anyhow, the situation should have been plain enough long ago without having to be spelled out in so many words. Aunt Ethel warned me and then I overheard Eva telling Jenise: I wish Jerome would stop following me around like a little dog. That's what she said. So Alex with his rose comb gets the girl. Combs, crests, wattles, plumes, horns—these are the things that matter.

Brisket, man, not so prime cut—that's what you are.

This is what the heart says (and this is all the heart says)— first *lub* (at the apex), then *dup* (at the valve closures). Occasionally a fluttering at the cusps and I flatter myself the earth shifts with the same giddy motion.

Everything seems reduced, diminished and paled. Or maybe

just normal after a high. Here we are, hoeing our little half-acres in rows and we call it a festival of creativity. My pseudo-pregnancy project seems nothing more than a little prank to me now. The picture is clear—rabbits mated with vasectomized males and rabbits mated with fertile males give a roughly parallel blood picture for up to thirteen days. The picture is clear, but what it means isn't in the least.

My adrenalectomy studies make a neat report. But I dream of other things. I want invariances, not correlations, and correlations are all I'm getting. I want laws. Most of what I'm doing is about as useful as establishing a connection between left-handedness and living in Detroit. There may be a correlation for all I know. So what if there is? Without an encompassing theory, a correlation is only an oddity, a goad. Trouble is, I have no large theoretical hunches, only little points of curiosity. I hunger for structure and certainty. A perfect candidate for faith, the Alkahest would say. And for him faith means premature closure, failure.

A teasing thought—here we are, rushing back and forth, experimenting madly, filled with importance. And yet *we* are the experiment.

Isaiah was dismissed late this evening. By the way the Elosons reckon, it was probably a long time coming. But by any reckoning it was cruel coming so late. He was at the stage of winding up all his projects. I don't think he made any appeal on his own behalf and this strikes me as strange, very strange. We tried to speak to Chief, a bunch of us, after the formal announcement of expulsion. But Chief refused to hear us out. We still plan to try and reach the Alkahest early tomorrow morning but I doubt it will be early enough. And I don't know what he would do or could do even if we did reach him. After all, the Elosons are in charge here at the Four Winds.

Naomi collected some money for Isaiah's ride to Boston. She asked me to take it up because she insisted he wasn't speaking to her any more. I told her I was sure that wasn't so, but I wasn't sure. I went upstairs. The bedroom door was closed. I knocked. Not a sound. I didn't bother to knock again. I opened the door. He was sitting on the edge of his bed. There was no sign of packing in progress.

I don't want any visitors, he said. Not even you, Jerome. I told Joel to tell you guys.

Well, I'm sorry, I said. For that and other things. We're trying to reach the Alkahest early tomorrow morning. There's a chance he might listen and step in. Just a chance—can you wait?

He shrugged.

In case it doesn't work out—Naomi said you needed some money for staying in Boston till things cooled down. Here. I put forward what I had.

He shooed my hand away.

It's a loan, I said. Accept it as a loan.

I won't be needing it. Changed my mind. I'll go direct.

Maybe more sensible, I said. But wait a little.

Got to face things sooner or later. Get a grip on myself, he said, looking me straight in the eye. Turn off the light—will you—when you go?

That was my cue to go.

I wanted to say something more, but the words died in my throat.

I switched off the light.

32

"SHH . . . LISTEN!"

"It's the wind. Go to sleep."

"Wind on the roof? Just listen."

Anna kept waking during the night, rattling the springs, making it impossible for Bob to sleep. "Now what?" he'd say, and Anna would keep on telling him there was someone on the roof. "Take an aspirin," he'd say, "and let me sleep. I don't hear a thing. You're out of your head."

She twisted and shifted, trying to find the magic position, but sleep wouldn't come. She recited all the odd names of birds she could remember, to be doing something: ruff, longspur, dovekie, gannet, shoveler, godwit, petrel, turnstone, veery, willet, bufflehead, loon, wheatear, stilt . . .

. . . skimmer, whimbrel, nuthatch, guillemot, flicker, redstart, veery . . . she'd said that before . . . grebe, grackle . . .

Grackle. Exactly what it sounded like. Steps . . .

For what seemed an interminable time, she held her breath and listened. Either her heart was beating outside her body or those were steps. Bob had fallen off at last and she didn't dare wake him.

Then it went dead quiet. Nothing but country sounds: crickets, branches stirring, a buoy slowly swinging.

Again: a heavy creaking, as though someone were forcing a door. Slowly and quietly, trying her best not to rock the bed, Anna slipped her feet to the floor. Then waited on the edge of the bed, holding her breath and trying her best not to move so as not to confuse the sounds she was hearing with her own sounds.

There *was* something.

A muffled crash, a faint bleat, mewling noises. It sounded like a sack of kittens. Anna peered down through the window, but the night was overcast, she couldn't see a thing.

It was perfectly quiet now. Only the sound of the ocean, calm, measured, a sleeper's breathing.

Sometime after that, she must have slept. But not for long. She woke feeling more exhausted than when she first stretched out. She went over to the window, trying to remember something, she couldn't think what. It was gray outside, a cold, low-hanging mist covered the early morning.

There was rain in the air, but none came down. A leaf flew upward. Something was lying in the driveway, near the hedge, a gray shape on a darker ground. Anna rubbed her eyes.

She returned to bed and was beginning to doze when she felt someone shaking and shaking her.

"Quick! Shh . . ." It was Bob. "I need you. There's been an accident. C'mon, get up! Grab your housecoat—no time to dress—come on."

She got up. She wished she hadn't.

The rising sun made a pale division in the sky. The grass was covered with webs, faint dew.

She knew who it was without looking. And that there was no chance of life in him. It was as if she had known all along what was coming.

He was lying on his side. One half of his face was finely beaded with the morning damp; the other was flush to the ground. His glasses lay at a distance. They seemed to be barely scratched. When Anna stooped to pick them up, a lens fell out and shivered into a hundred fine fragments. "An eye is shaped in darkness to receive the light," she remembered. Something Dr. Alkavist once said: "A labor of eons . . . an eye is formed."

Bob went off in search of Chief; he left Anna in charge, with instructions to ward off the students.

She stood there, her back to the dead boy, unaware that she was still clutching the frame of his glasses. She kept thinking, wishing that at least he had jumped the other way. If he had made the water, it would have been cleaner. It was cold, bitch cold. A group of students passed her at a distance of yards. They were picking their way along the path, making a clatter with their mops and pails, and ragging Eddy, who must have been only half awake. The cleaning crew was starting earlier every day.

No one thought to ask what Anna was doing out so early, standing there in a thin housecoat, standing so still.

They passed. All clear.

Not so clear. A few minutes later, Naomi shot through the door. She cleared the porch steps in a single bound. She was late and signaled to Anna: had the others gone? Anna pointed to the Mouse House, a perfectly clear and unambiguous signal. Why then was Naomi veering from the path and racing toward her?

"*That* way!" Anna hollered, but there was no stopping her.

"I wonder whether Mr. Homay . . ." Naomi's voice trailed off. She stared for a little. "He asked to borrow some money last night. I didn't think—"

"I'm sure that had nothing to do with it," Anna said firmly. "I'm going to ask you to go back to the house and wait for the bell. Promise not to say anything about this before Chief does."

Naomi nodded.

"You all right?"

Bob came up, Alfred behind him, lugging a heavy tarpaulin. Then Chief, who knelt down close to the body. Anna looked away. "We'll have to call an ambulance anyway," Chief said. He noticed Naomi. "My God, will you get that girl out of here?"

The bells started soon afterwards. They rang without pause for several minutes. It was a new signal, an alarming one, and all the students came on the run. They gathered in the common room. Chief didn't have but a minute or two to talk to them, to state that there had been no pain.

"Out like a light," he promised them. He advised the students to busy themselves with their usual tasks, as far as they were able. His voice was small and he swallowed words. A smoke would have steadied his hands, but he didn't seem to think of it.

Less than an hour later the body was pronounced officially dead and carted off. The police had come. "Disease, accident, homicide, suicide—there are no other ways," the officer said. "Which will it be?" He seemed to be offering a choice.

Naomi wanted to be alone. She eluded Joel and found herself back on the path she had taken on her first morning. She retraced her circuit until she came to the escarpment where she'd spotted— She passed quickly by, and went on retracing her steps until she came to the cliff's edge. She studied the ledge and the sea beneath for some time, time out of mind, in a kind of cessation. No thoughts, nothing she could call grief, she felt nothing— just shivery. She noticed with some surprise that the sun had broken through the mist. It was a warm sun, already the rocks were warming to the touch.

Three bells sounded: it must have been lunchtime. Naomi decided to ignore the summons. Three bells, four winds, four hundred eels—was it a code of some kind? She'd lost the clear pattern of the summer.

Aunt Ethel did not appear that day. Everyone was left to his or her own devices. The only one who seemed to know what she was doing was Tertu. If she muttered in the kitchen, no one heard. Meals were served on schedule.

Some of the students took turns sitting with the Homay children while Bob and Anna assisted Chief with the endless protocol of death. It was Bob Homay who handled the long-distance calls. He emerged very pale from one of them, and spent several minutes pacing the corridor before he confronted the phone again. The funeral would be held in New York. Only the immediate family.

Sue and Jim had a day of it. "We're doing fine, just fine," Eva assured Anna.

Continuous diversion, anyway. They played spit, war and I-doubt-it. They kept up a game of jacks for hours. Eva was an old pro. Passing through the hall, Anna heard her calling out:

"Cart!"

"Mother's helper."

"Interference—no fair! That's it. Foursies for me!" Called out with more volume and gusto than any game of jacks warranted. And when Anna got back to her room in time for the napping hour, she found that Susie had made Magic-Marker tattoos—no pattern but twisting lines—all over her left arm. It was hard to fool children.

Bob and Anna spent the rest of the day in search of some sort of note which would explain everything. One worked down the east wing, one the west. They took the house room by room, floor by floor. Whenever they crossed paths, they kissed. They kissed in and they kissed out. Their past quarrels seemed small and foolish. Suddenly life seemed very frail, terribly precious.

"Where is that note?" Chief asked again and again, convinced that a note existed somewhere. Bob knew that, statistically, it wasn't so: not all suicides left notes. Many left nothing at all. But there was no talking to Chief. The Homays turned the house upside down for clues. Joel assisted as best he could. They found two envelopes under Isaiah's pillow; both were sealed. The Homays hesitated for a moment. Then Joel tore them open: *Hello. How are you? Birthday greetings.*

The Homays lifted and poked, Joel went down on his hands and knees, but they found nothing helpful. A single sneaker, a stick of rosin, score paper, a tube of medicinal paste for adolescent skin—these were the only notes. He'd made no effort to pack. They discovered his fiddle stashed away with the luggage in the basement. It hadn't been touched in days. The case was already lightly mantled with dust.

Defeat only seemed to reinforce Chief's conviction. By dinner time, he was certain that the note was in some ever-so-obvious place, so obvious that everyone was bound to overlook it. He was also convinced that the note would contain a confession that Isaiah had been on drugs. To Anna, this was the clearest index of Chief's desperation. He kept harping on it. At least a note to Isaiah's father, that *had* to be. There was a ragged edge of hysteria to Chief's voice, and the Homay's urged him to go in to Aunt Ethel and lie down for an hour.

But Chief wouldn't lie down.

By nine that evening, Anna could have written the note herself.

At ten to eleven, Anna quit. She went into Chief's study to tell him. He was sitting at his long desk; his glasses were folded and his eyes were puffy. "I don't know why he did it," he whispered. "He couldn't have done more to sabotage us. Tell me, Anna, where did we go wrong?" He really seemed to want to know.

Anna fell into bed without brushing her teeth. Bob was already lying in darkness. They remained stretched out, side by side, neither touching nor speaking, filled with the strangeness of the day past. Anna remembered the sound of kittens, and then she remembered nothing.

For the next few days the students managed on their own. They continued working on their final reports, although deadlines were in abeyance and the old urgency was gone. The work crews met and went through their paces, paying meticulous attention to detail, though certain that no one would inspect them. Routine was a drug and a welcome one. The students clung to the sense of stability which a fixed schedule gave them.

Chief was occupied, always in some other part of the house. Although he was "on call," no one called him. He dined alone. He ate quickly and was out of the room well before the dish crew came in to clear.

Bob Homay was everywhere, available and willing.

For two days Aunt Ethel slept. There was much speculation. The word "breakdown" was rumored about in undertones—the sort of word the students normally would have rejected, clouded as it was in imprecision, and steeped in melodrama. All they could say with confidence was that Aunt Ethel was sleeping, under sedation, very likely, and that the Elosons quarters were strictly off-limits.

On the third evening after the accident, the entire household met in the common room. Aunt Ethel was present, her first appearance since the accident. The question at issue was whether the graduation ceremonies should go forward as planned. Dr. Alkavist presided.

He spoke without ceremony, above a low hissing and buzzing.

"My friends."

Silence. Dr. Alkavist cleared his throat.

Once again: "My friends, let us observe a moment of silence in memory of Isaiah Yettman, a gifted boy, a headstrong boy, a boy too young to . . ." To? The last word was inaudible, inadmissible. Then he did something Anna never expected: Dr. Alkavist, proud Promethean, inclined, no—bowed, his head.

A pause. A moment of silence. What to think of?

The petitions, the scolds, have floated off him at last, Anna thought. Why not leave the boy alone? She bowed her head and studied her lap as if in church, not knowing what to do, not daring to look around. She thought of Isaiah, she thought of the name but couldn't focus on what she remembered of the boy; his acne, his too-quick, staccato speech, his glasses always crusted. Then she remembered the sounds he made when tuning up his fiddle. She heard him quite clearly softly singing *sol* down to *do*, tuning the A string, then D, then—

Chief cleared his throat. "No point dwelling on the past," he said. "What's done is done. The past is regretted. There's no point saying how much. The point is—what are we going to do now?" Would the Director come to the point? Without any fine phrases. No more poetry, please. There was an electric crackle in Chief's voice, brittle sparks of tension shooting off from a frayed wire.

The dead, the deed, the done. Anna had slept heavily but badly, and stumbled through the day thick with weariness. She'd been haunted by odd thoughts like: What do milk and sulk have in common? And odd expressions like "sea cucumbers," "hammertoes," and "hush money." Only that morning, she heard Susie jumping to a rhyme she'd never heard before:

> A tisket, a tasket,
> Someone's in his casket.

Skip, skip, skip. She was keeping brisk time.

"The point is." The point? Dr. Alkavist looked vague, as if he'd momentarily forgotten what the call to meeting was about. Stalling, he began to cashier lint from his sleeve.

The point? Again, a low buzzing. Dr. Alkavist made a gavel of his plastic waterglass, tapped with great energy, with a shallow sound, then, as if faint, sagged against the lectern.

The buzzing. He straightened, filled his glass, took a sip of water, then dabbed his lips with a handkerchief. Would the cracked voice carry? With the same handkerchief, he wiped his glasses, misted them, wiped them. He slipped his glasses on, frowned: no better. With the same handkerchief, he blew his nose. He stared at the students: are you real? His eyes moved over the crowd, taking the separate faces in, pausing over shades of difference glimpsed for the first time. He seemed to recognize no one. Was it real? Was it a dream? Was the dream so cunning?

"Why won't he begin?" Stevie muttered.

A few seconds more of this and Herb, ever a practical fellow, would rush in to fill the vacuum.

"My friends . . ."

At last. What was it he used to say? "Ladies and gentlemen, respected colleagues, students—" Something like that. Everyone in their places, all neatly ranked and ordered less than a week before. Now all in disarray.

He broached the issue. Should they hold the graduation as planned? Or, in view of the tragic, unforeseen circumstances, should they forgo the ceremony and the festivities? Or should they observe only the ceremony without the festivities?

Herb advocated "a reasonable compromise." The festivities should, of course, be cancelled. "No one's much in the mood now," he admitted. But the certificate-granting ceremony should proceed on schedule. Canceling the ceremony would be unfair to those who worked so hard to complete their projects. Even more important, it would harm the program, dishonor the idea, the founding dream.

Stevie corroborated. Science waits for no man—that was the gist of it. Science marches on. Individuals pass, institutions remain. We must not give in to the forces of obstruction.

Forces of obstruction? My God, Anna thought.

Aunt Ethel shifted in her chair as though about to speak. Anna waited for her to rise and claim the lectern as usual, but it did not happen. Aunt Ethel simply sat and nodded to herself. Once, a small bubble formed at the corner of her lips, her throat strained, and Anna felt certain—*now* she would begin. But again Aunt Ethel's head fell, chin slumped to collarbone, and she seemed to doze.

Eva held the floor: "How would giving up the ceremony serve to honor the memory of Isaiah?" Rhetorical question. "It would honor no one."

All salved over? So fast? You can airbrush anything, anything at all, Anna concluded, and make it look good.

"Life does not go on as before," Jerome struck the one discordant note. "If Isaiah doesn't matter, then none of us matters. And the group can't matter because nothing plus nothing is nothing."

Aunt Ethel nodded to Jerome as she had to Stevie and to Herb before him; she nodded to the defense, she nodded to the prosecution. Then she jolted awake and stared, dull-eyed, at the chair ahead. She seemed terribly white and rickety, smaller than remembered. How had a woman so pathetically frail brought everyone to their knees as she had? As she had! As she continued to do, even in half-sleep, an effigy of herself.

Vito asked for a secret ballot, still apparently fearful of reprisal or at least pressure.

They voted.

It was eleven to five to continue the ceremony as scheduled, canceling the festivities. There were three abstentions. Who were the dissidents? Anna felt sure she could figure it out if only she thought hard enough, but she couldn't think at all at the moment.

A few details remained. Again Anna tried to think of Isaiah, and again she failed. He was a boy, unformed. Not yet a man. He should have been more patient.

A committee was appointed to decide how to decorate the common room, whether to garland the fireplace with flowers or ferns, whether a speech in memoriam should be given, or only passing mention.

33

THE PACKING yet to be done—Anna would be at it all day. She'd have to be finished before seven; that was when the ceremony was scheduled. The Homays planned to leave early the next morning. No point hanging around. They'd see what summer they could salvage on their way back home—not much, but something.

Where had they accumulated all this? Had things expanded when she unpacked? Everything from boots and ski sweaters to bathing suits and shorts, enough for three seasons. Sometimes they'd run through three seasons all in the same day.

She hadn't seen Bart in quite a while. It was hard to tell when the last time had been. He must have gone off with the rest of the summer crowd. A pity. The ocean had been putting on quite a show these past few days, steaming and hissing, whipping up a lather. Bart would have loved it.

Bob had taken the children to town for a last round of

miniature golf. The students were at Spemann Lab for their final conferences. The house was empty, yet echoing, rumoring . . . a shell emptied of the sea.

Anna supposed the Elosons were packing, too. Beyond that, she didn't speculate, she couldn't. They hung out together, survivors. They were mild and pleasant, subdued, impersonal. Chief said something about longing to get back to Boston, "to a regular life."

Everybody going.

Nine fearfully intense weeks and Anna had learned— had she learned anything? Morals, extractions, the meaning of it all? The meaning? Too much to ask. She perceived, she suffered, really she didn't learn much. Whenever she tried to give advice, her own words came out like someone being dubbed.

After the body was carted away, Bob had wept. It was this reluctant confession of defeat which endeared Bob to her in the end, always. People "meant well," that was his conviction; when it had to be faced that they didn't, he wept. Weeping, his tears erased the evidence: people still meant well.

At least *Bob* meant well. For what it was worth.

Strange, that Anna had not mourned at all. She could not, would not, think of Isaiah. For a day or two she could not bear to watch the students eat, and in the evenings the silence weighed upon her, but nothing more.

At summer's end, patterns had clearly formed, lives had taken shape, and Anna could foresee many things. Hans Tivonen, with steady work and luck, would be a Nobel laureate someday. His sponsor was counting on it. Eva would marry early, have children, and almost surely drop her career. Polly and Joel would become geneticists, their interests were already sharply defined. Tom Li would be a surgeon, one of the best.

Isaiah would be—what he had already become.

And Naomi? There Anna's vision failed.

"All fades . . ." Who said that? It didn't matter who, it was so. How it is, she thought, just how it is. Simple economy: there isn't enough time for it to be otherwise. Like now, take this very moment. No time for anything but the problem at hand. Here were three cartons already full. How she'd ever get it squared away was beyond her, even with most of the suitcases going to the carrier on the roof of the car— Not *her* problem, thank goodness. Loading the car was Bob's headache.

Now here was a sorry mess! How did Bob's lumber jacket ever come to this? Looked like he slept in an alley—lint, burrs, tufts of rabbit hair. It was his warmest, he'd need it on the road early in the morning. Too late to get it cleaned, she'd see what she could do. Pluck it like any daisy—how did that rhyme go? "One I love, two I love, three I love I say, four I love with all my heart, five I cast away . . ."

34

Naomi's summer projects were concluded, observations duly recorded. If she'd harvested anything that summer, it was questions, more questions than she'd started with—no answers. She'd kept her tissue explants alive (you could call it life) in a state of static equilibrium for fifty days. There'd been no cell wandering and no growth in the sense of differentiation and articulation. The explants spread out as epithelial sheets with no development of the basal portions of the ear. Naomi had some thoughts on the limitations of her present techniques, some thoughts for future improvement.

Nothing conclusive or even faintly compelling had emerged from her first investigations into the eating habits of genetically obese mice. In the little time she'd been able to observe them, she'd noted that the normal mice tended to eat a fairly constant volume of food and had responded to dilution by increasing intake. They'd also shown some periodicity in their eating habits, as if responding to a hunger "drive." But the obese mice had shown no such tendencies; they'd nibbled constantly, shown a proportionally smaller increase in their intake of diluted food, nothing constant or regular. These fat ones reminded Naomi a little of animals called "filter feeders," of whales or even of clams, who fed without effort or desire, small bits of food and the world sweeping through them continually. An exaggeration—but the evidence, tentative and patchy as it was, tended to suggest a clear, felt hunger drive in normal mice and something formless in the obese.

She was finished. On Thursday the student reports were submitted and gathered up in spring binders, one book per student. Joel and Chief worked together on a volume for Isaiah. The spine of each binder was lettered in white ink with the name of the student, the year, and the uniform title *Reports*. Then the books were delivered over to the library of Spemann Lab, where, unless something came up, they'd be covered with dust and forgotten.

"My, how you've grown up," Naomi's mother said quietly, not unsatisfied with the changes. Grown up—was that what it was?

A day and a night and everything went round. Trying to recapture her life before she came to the Four Winds, Naomi couldn't grasp the thread. Those years, those months before, had passed in a kind of sleep. It was like a song, a strange haunting song, a maybe-beautiful song, caught in the car radio while passing through a strange town. Then: a tunnel. The ending and the name of the song are lost forever. You jiggle the dial frantically but it's no use: you can't recapture, you'll never reconnect.

Riddle: I eat the road I travel by. What's my name?
Answer: Time

It was the first time she'd ever seen a dead person. A thoracic hump—that's all there was. Naomi had seen plenty of dead animals before and this was the same, the same and different. He looked like he knew something and was trying to tell it—or cry out with it. That was what made the difference. His mouth was open with no sound coming out.

"You kids sure accomplished a lot," some proud parent said above the crowd.

She'd accomplished, yes, she'd accomplished. She'd successfully completed her projects, all she set out to do.

When she came to say goodbye to Joel, it wasn't as wrenching as she'd expected. The real wrench had come before. In many ways, Naomi was looking forward to going home, to slowing down for a while. Joel agreed to meet her in the city over Thanksgiving recess. Naomi wasn't convinced that they would really get together then, or ever, but the planning eased them. They exchanged their certificates as soon as they received them. It was partly a gesture like exchanging rings, and partly a nose-thumbing at pretension, at achievement too. The high cost of achievement. They weren't thinking of the years ahead, that it might be nice someday to look back, to find some memento of a summer spent without diversions, of a time when time was used to the fullest, a summer of the mind.

Jerome had already gone. He'd phoned his parents and left on Friday evening. It was the evening before the ceremony, and he let it be known that he left in protest. "Life does not go on as before," he said, "not for me, anyway." His name was read out and Alex Nesselroth, who followed him in the alphabet, accepted the certificate in Jerome's place. Later, it would be sent to him. The Elosons had little use for this kind of gesture.

There were no festivities, as they had all agreed beforehand. The lectern was full of white flowers. The Alkahest gave a very moving speech in memoriam. "Death is no terminus," he told them. Around Isaiah, he spun a tale. A tale that sounded like program notes to a grand opera: he is not dead, only sleeping. The poison he took was not poison. The word the Alkahest used most was "*Aufhebung*," which nobody understood, even though he kept translating it as "a binding up and a raising." It was all lost on his audience, the kind of thing only Jerome might have understood and believed, and Jerome was miles away.

Jerome had turned belligerent after the incident. He'd gone around challenging one student after another: "Name one thing you believe with certainty, just one thing."

Most of the students shrugged their shoulders and looked vague. "What's this—Dostoyevsky?" Leo sounded angry. "You want to know what I think of God? I'll tell you. When I think of God, I think of a kind of gas with lights in it, winking lights."

Joel was one of the few who took Jerome seriously. "Here's one thing I believe: within a hundred years we'll all be dead."

"And on that rock, what foundations can you build?"

"Build? What should I build? What are you talking about? I can live without certainty—I've got to. Anyhow, I haven't any prejudices."

"No prejudices, no convictions, either," Jerome summed it up.

It was Chief's turn to speak. He addressed himself to the problems and challenges confronting young people in the difficult days ahead. He spoke at length about the tragedy of drug abuse wasting the best resources of the nation's youth. As always, he spoke without naming names and yet seeming to. Without pause or transition, he mentioned that negotiations were in progress with the Board of Trustees to set up a scholarship in Isaiah's name.

The students took this in silently.

Then he spoke to them about "the human prospect." He spoke in the grand manner they had come to associate with the Alkahest, but the message was less glowing. He doled out a certain amount of despair, a certain amount of hope—a particle more of hope, and sent the students forth to do battle.

He gripped the lectern as he spoke, pressed his palms against the wood, as if grateful for its solidity.

There were refreshments afterwards, fruit punch, and party sandwiches, looking dainty with the crusts trimmed off. Tertu had done her best to make an elegant spread. Aunt Ethel appeared briefly at the reception. She stood off to one side in a gray-green dress, harmonizing quietly with two rose ladies on her left and one vermilion on her right. She listened attentively but spoke little. Chief went over and stood alongside her, he put his arm around her shoulder. It was a thing carefully done. She turned to him gratefully. Among the sponsors, Dr. Kamin was conspicuous by his absence.

Naomi had never been to a party like this one. People smiled, stretched their cheeks, and showed their teeth, but they never raised their voices and no one laughed aloud. In undertones, they mentioned "the awful tragedy." All the guests felt obliged to mention it at least once in passing, but no one dwelled upon it. People chatted and milled around for an hour and then it was over. It was like putting a million fireflies end to end, trying to make a sunset.

Lebret shook her hand twice, said that he hoped Naomi would go on, and asked her to keep in touch. "There are so many questions—we're just beginning to master a few of the technical problems, then we'll begin, building up from simples." He made her promise never to forget Occam's razor, whatever that was—some inscription engraved on a razor? Something about not making explanations more complicated than necessary. "*Entia non sunt multiplicanda . . .*" he said it very slowly. Naomi wondered why Lebret was disregarding his own advice and making such a *megillah* about something so obvious. She wondered whether it wasn't a sly dig at Chief's elaborate accountings for recent events and the Alkahest's embroideries of everything.

Before they broke up, the students presented the Elosons with a photo album they'd put together more than two weeks before. It was called *MacPherson at the Four Winds*. MacPherson was a cartoon mouse. Stevie had drawn him in the bottom lefthand corner of every other page, pointing and gesturing. The album was full of everybody's photos, full of memories. The captions read:

> At Fuller's garden
> Scalpels poised!
> "Where's that clamp?!!!"
> Cake
> All the little Homays
> Aunt Ethel and Ao
> Forceps—OOPS!
> Seventh inning

They went on like that—breezy little banners under the gray and white. There were photos of each and every member of the group, and more than anyone else of Chief in surgical garb, dramatically masked and gloved—Chief in his element. There was a photo of Vito strumming his unused tennis racket like a guitar, a photo of Tom Li goldbricking, lounging on a table in the Rabbit House and wielding his mop by remote control.

Somewhere in the midst of all those photos, on a page the Elosons didn't notice in flipping through, there was a picture of Isaiah standing in the empty lecture hall. It wasn't the sharpest photo in the world, though Bob Homay snapped it, and he was a fine photographer. Still, it was clearly Isaiah. It must have been early evening, the light insufficient.

He was standing in the empty lecture hall, back to the window, torso swaying. His face was half in shadow, everything followed the dip of his bowing arm. His quick fingers were entirely blurred by motion.

There was no caption under this picture.

About the Author

A. G. Mojtabai was born in Brooklyn in 1937. She graduated from Antioch College in 1958 with a B.A. in philosophy and a minor in mathematics.

Soon after graduation, Ms. Mojtabai married and moved to Iran, where she lived with her husband in a large extended family. They later moved with their two children to Karachi, Pakistan, and then to Lahore.

When she returned to the United States in 1967 Ms. Mojtabai did graduate work at Columbia University, receiving an M.A. in philosophy in 1968 and an M.S. in library science in 1970. She lectured in philosophy for two years at Hunter College and is now a librarian at City College. Ms. Mojtabai lives in New York City with her daughter; she finished *The 400 Eels of Sigmund Freud* at Yaddo last summer and is now at work on a third novel.